Tru Untrue

RACHELLE JONES SMITH

Summary: Tru moves from the city to the suburbs where a scrutinizing teacher threatens to uncover his past. With graduation on the line, he pairs with the ostracized Nell for a project. Can she keep his secret while he helps her to find her voice and repair the rift in her family?

[1. Family problems – Fiction. 2. Sexual identity – Fiction. 3. Gender norms – Fiction. 4. Schools – Fiction. 5. High schools – Fiction. 6. Poetry - Fiction. 7. Identity – Fiction.]

Library of Congress Cataloging-in-Publication Data
Jones Smith, Rachelle.
Tru Untrue/ by Rachelle Jones Smith
2020900237

ISBN 978-0-578-61884-5 Paperback
ISBN978-0-578-62544-7 Hardcover

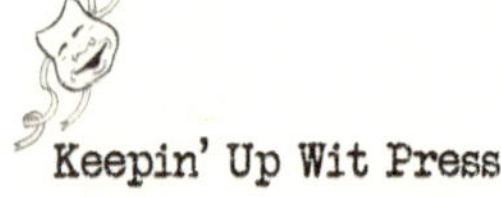

Keepin' Up Wit Press

Tru Untrue

For those who wear the masks because the world isn't ready to see their truths.
And for my family, who lets me live my truest.

Exist
escape
truth
TRU
LAUGH!
future
hide the pain
who hurt you?
CLO WN
Save
POETIC SOUL
they're
laughing
who is she?
AT YOU
WHERE IS SHE?
PAST
#pride
Always
LOVE
Live your truth

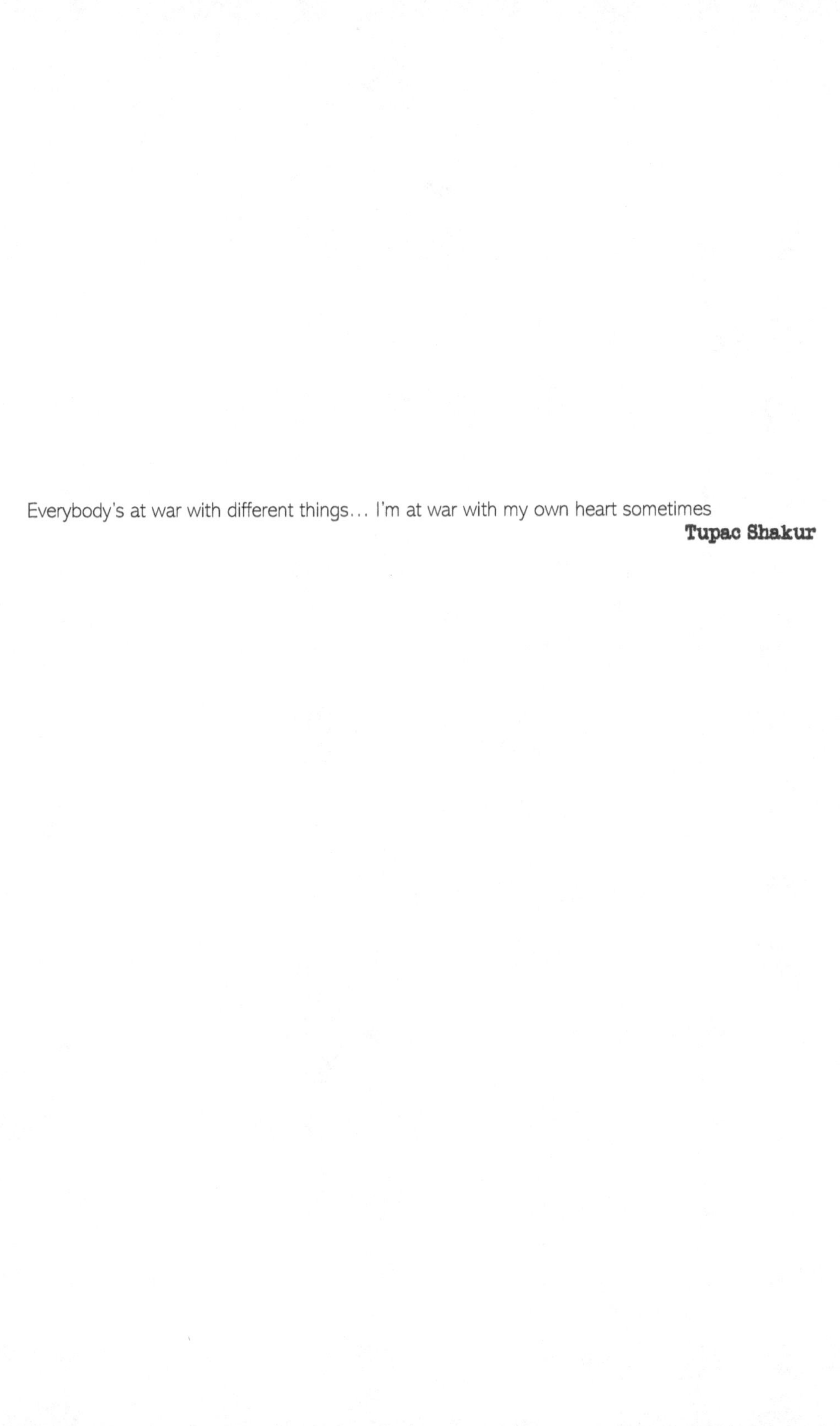

Everybody's at war with different things… I'm at war with my own heart sometimes

Tupac Shakur

Tru

She's gonna come for me in five... four... three... two...

"Tru! Once again I have nothing from you, " Ms. Yashar begins her rant and I'm trying my best to feign attention. I realize late that I've missed some of her lecture, tuned her out. I try to focus. "...every time. Are you planning to graduate? You're not acting like it. You know this class is required, right? Tru?"

She's waiting for a reply, but I learned day one to let her finish, so she's awkwardly standing over me at the side of my desk as though proximity were some sort of intimidation tactic. There's nothing about Ms. Yashar to make me - or anyone else - nervous. I inhale her cinnamon and flower scent and nearly gag on its intensity.

I sit straighter in my chair. "I got the assignment here, Ms. Y. You know, computer issues. Can't catch a break with the 'net."

She drums manicured fingers on my desk. Truncating her name is a no. So is bouncing to the odd little beat she's tapping, but I cannot help it.

"Tru, I think you're full of it. Every day there's an excuse. And not one is plausible."

She turns and walks to her desk without touching my work. Lips pursed, she avoids looking at me and taps her keyboard. I know she's punched an F into the gradebook.

"Aww, come on. I'm *Tru*-full. The work's done and it's right here for you." I widen my eyes like those puppies and kittens in the pictures and press the palm of one hand to my chest.

The class snickers at my joke. Ms. Yashar flushes, her face flashes - is it anger? - and I see her suck in her breath. Okay, not funny, Tru. *Chill.*

I'm not fixin' to tell her *why* I can't do this digital classroom she insists on. She's not exactly one of those concerned teachers, anyway. It's been like this since I joined the class three weeks ago.

Midyear transfers aren't easy, but mine was a necessity. Nope, my pops is not military - I don't know what he does. He hasn't been a part of my life since creation. From what I've heard, he chased my mom for months before she acknowledged his existence. It was a game of tag for him, except after she was *it*, he split. And Ma isn't one to chase back. She's a strong single lady, my Ma. Always has been. Pops was gone before she knew I was truly coming. That's probably why she named me ... he'd lied so much trying to gain her trust that she gifted me a little honesty for my birth day. And here I am, joining a "regularly scheduled program already in progress" in my senior year.

I know it sounds like I'm a statistic — like I'm from some broken family that moves around when rent's due or something — but that's not me. Ma's never let her household break. I'm the reason we had to move. It was my trouble that stuck me here.

Ms. Yashar was caught off guard when she first saw me. She'd been out of the classroom when I walked in. I got my schedule in the office and first block was English, room 210. The halls were crowded when that warning bell rang. I dodged quite a few short kids running - actually running - to their classes. Must've been freshmen. The rest of the students seemed to be on the slowest march in history and I stumbled a bit to move so slow. I'm 6'1" and long legs travel briskly. Side-stepping the sauntering masses, I made it to the room well before the tardy bell, picked an empty chair in the first row by the door and the white board, and took out my notebook. First impressions, right?

Naw. It didn't matter that I was prompt and ready. Ms. Yashar arrived right after the bell ceased its piercing cry. Every seat in the room was occupied and the chatter was deafening. She stopped in the doorway, eyes on me and face contorted like an obnoxious odor had reached her nose at the threshold of the class. I guess she wasn't expecting late editions to her course?

She fixed her face into a forced smile. Taking the few steps to my desk, she stood in front of me, sizing me up.

"And you are?"

She was barely my height while I sat at my desk, so her eyes looked directly into mine.

"Tru Pitre. I'm in this class now."

"Hmm. I didn't get notice I'd have another new student." She said it quietly, more to herself than to me. Then after a pause, she looked at her other students. I took the opportunity to look closer at Ms. Yashar. She was maybe thirty, and despite the bags under her dark colored eyes, she was attractive. Her voice rose to match the conversations around us. "Quiet. The bell rang. It's my time, not social hour. Notebooks out." Another pause, then directly to me, "Well, welcome to Language Arts, Tru."

"Thanks," I said, flashing my *I'm so charming* smile. She smiled back, and this time it looked genuine. I counted it as a minor success. If she likes me even a little, I have a chance in this class. I'm pretty good at English, even dabble in writing lines. And I read -- English teachers like that. I shift my notebook a bit to make sure she can see my favorite book, *The Rose That Grew from Concrete*, is also on my desk. She may not know 'Pac, but she'll know I come with my own reading material.

That first class was uneventful, but Ms. Yashar clearly didn't want any more students on her roster. She ignored me the remainder of that block. I guess she figured I'd catch on to the assignments without her explanation.

"Don't forget to read the chapter and post responses to the following question on our digital board." She wrote our writing prompt in a scrawling cursive on the white board, then she turned to me, as she seemed to remember my invasion. "Tru – I've printed out the instructions. You do have a computer, right?"

"Uh..." I started to answer, but the bell diverted Ms. Yashar's attention as the class rose as one and rushed the exit. Just my luck that I get the tech savvy teacher. This online thing was going to be a serious problem. I joined the student exodus without finishing my response.

The span of classes since then has been a series of diversions and stalling. I've gotten good at it and teach is my biggest fan, I'm sure of it. Some of my performances have been inspired. Some have landed me in the office. Same class, same digital post assignment, different day.

"Tru?" Ms. Yashar begins. It's always a public address. I see Claire, the red-haired cheerleader with the piercing blue eyes, begin to laugh.

Soon, her whole squad is laughing with her. I'm figuring they already find this daily lecture amusing at my expense, so why not give them something to laugh about?

The show begins. "Yes'm?"

"You didn't post your assigned entry again." Ms. Yashar emphasizes the *again* with a disgruntled *humph*. She's staring at me hard and one eyebrow is raised like she's auditioning her smolder to play a relative of The Rock.

Something about her tells me she's not a huge wrestling fan, so I resist the urge to tell her that I, too, *smell what The Rock is cooking.*

Instead, I conjure up a little Charlie Chaplin. I'm quite the silent film aficionado, so my repertoire is full, and Chaplin (writer, director, *and* composer) is golden. Chaplin doesn't talk much, but he is hella expressive.

I rake my hand through my hair, messing up my twists so they fall in my face. I blow them out my eyes with a louder-than-needed side-of-the-mouth *pfft*. I raise my eyebrows (I'm thinking this is my coy 'What did I do wrong?' look). Quick shoulder shrug. Dramatic pockets check starting with the fronts, which I pull inside out, then standing slew-foot beside my chair, I pat the back pockets. Another shrug. Lips pursed. Eyebrow wiggle. Finger point and wagging hand to signal my *ahah*! Then, I waddle penguin-like a la Chaplin around the front of my desk to my backpack (though going behind my chair would've been quicker). I pretend the zipper is stuck, then fake-tugging, I open the bag to reveal my plastic folder. I peak inside, casting nervous glances around as though ensuring no one can see the contents.

At this point, the whole class is watching my performance. The laughter becomes my soundtrack.

Then, as I hear the quick, angry clicking of Ms. Yashar's heels coming toward me, I whip out a handwritten sheet and wave it triumphantly toward her. Full teeth smile. End scene.

She's pissed. Snatching the paper from my hand, she points to the door without a word. She's joined my silent film cast!

I look at her and break character, "Me?" In my head, I see the typed caption, but she can't see that, so I have to say it.

She's standing at the front of the classroom ignoring me as she instructs the rest of the class to stop laughing and get into their literature circles. Desks are scraping the tile floor and people are shuffling into place as I bid *adieu* with a flamboyant bow at the door.

Repeat her beratement on each subsequent assignment. Duplicate the laughing classmates. Change up my performance, though I must admit that Chaplin receives the best reactions. There you have it – Ms. Yashar's English 12 class for nearly a month. And she still hasn't asked why I won't - why I *can't* do her digital class. It's not in my file, if she even bothered to look. As long as I finish my community service and get the dividends together to right my wrong, nothing but the press coverage will remain. *Tabula rasa.* Minors don't have their names printed and Ma insisted we leave the old 'hood to start a new story.

Nell

She needed to escape. The class was just beginning and already it was obvious that "language arts" - as Ms. Yashar insisted her class be called – would be *nothing* artistic beyond Nell's doodling to keep from drooling with boredom.

Ms. Yashar scribbled on the white board the day's agenda: Franz Kafka's *Metamorphosis*. Nell jotted down the topic in her mauve moleskin in swirling calligraphy. Ms. Yashar continued writing out the plans: journal, reading, discussion on perspective. Then she inhaled once, posed with her hands on her hips in front of the class, and started her lecture.

As Ms. Yashar rattled on about conformity, Nell concentrated on her sketch book. She was busy drawing a fly that had settled on the edge of her page. He seemed content there, first rubbing his arms together as though plotting some plan to torment the classroom, then smoothing the many delicate hairs on his head and between his protruding eyes, then sliding his back legs against one another. It didn't seem to mind Nell's pencil movements as she sketched his tiny features. It was as though he were posing for her while she zoned out of the monotonous lecture. How fitting, little bug, that you joined me while she's obsessing over Metamorphosis and the man who became an insect. Are you just like every other fly? I doubt it. There's something about you that is uniquely you, and I bet you work damn hard to ensure everyone knows that special spark.

Finally, after several minutes grooming himself on Nell's moleskin, his wings bounced slightly and spread, and he was gone.

What did Ms. Yashar know about being different? Her clothes were lifted from the pages of *InStyle* – each fitted sweater, silk blouse, or flowing skirt, each pair of high heels emulating the fashion spreads (if they weren't the exact pieces mentioned in the articles, which Nell suspected they were). Her hair, meticulously styled and colored with the popular Balayage technique, reflected the models'. And she was acutely aware of her makeup, checking her appearance several times a class as though compelled to ensure her eyeliner, shadow and long, thick lashes were on fleek. She actually used that word, believing herself in-the-know about her students' slang.

She doesn't remember what it's like to find herself. In the years past Ms. Yashar's youth, she likely buried the memories of seeking inclusion from peers. Who would dwell on the awkward, judgmental years of junior high?

Her portrait subject gone, Nell was suddenly aware of the people around her. The class buzzed with conversation and movement. Next to Nell, Carrie and – Nell had to think awhile to conjure the girl's name, then she remembered it – Sue failed at attempts to whisper their evening plans. *I bet*, Nell thought, *they're doing that for my benefit so I know what I'm missing.*

Brody was flipping through his college prospective. He'd been planning to attend an Ivy league school for as long as Nell could remember. In fact, he was in direct competition with her for valedictorian, though it was an honor she hardly cared about earning.

In the corner, Mason scrolled on his phone, periodically double-tapping with his index finger; he was nodding approvals for postings and he smirked every time he "liked" something – no doubt in anticipation of some girl's response to his virtual attention. Typical. Gathering the most attention on your carefully crafted online image was all that mattered to a lot of students.

Nelson, Micah, Nickie and Em sat upright and attentive in front desks, journals open and pens waiting for the day's confession assignment. They were always ready and willing to accommodate Ms. Yashar's whims without complaint or hesitation. These were her favorite students: overly attentive and obnoxiously compliant. Each one of them lived for Ms. Yashar's favor and she doted on them every class without fail.

Nell hadn't realized she was surveying until Jay caught her eyes. He smiled broadly at her. Shifting her gaze, she tried to appear unaware by making her face a_blank and oblivious mask. She didn't dare look up too soon, focusing instead on embellishing her notebook. *It's better to be invisible.*

Finally, Ms. Yashar revealed her prompt of the day. "I'm excited about this one," she said as she twirled toward them, her pleated skirt swirling around her legs. "We are influenced by our personal histories. They – the events of our lives – make us who we are and shape our perspectives..." she rattled on for several minutes, as it was common for her prompts to serve as lectures on life.

No. Not another reflection prompt. How does that connect to Kafka's guy waking up as a bug, anyway?

Nell held her breath. She couldn't – simply could not write about her personal life. The events that shaped her – that define her to her core – were too recent and too painful. She just would not share the intimate details of her ever-invading thoughts of Aidan no matter how well meaning the teacher thought she was being.

Nell fished through her pen pouch for a few colors, settling on four. She flipped to a fresh page and sketched an outstretched palm. Then she added flames engulfing the hand. Aidan. His name was Gaelic like her own. She was "champion" and he was "fire." Aidan had said it meant he was powerful and accomplished. He wore the name like an honor badge.

It was the only gift their parents gave that they couldn't shame away. Her father put Aidan through hell fire on earth.

She sketched fervently as Ms. Yashar finished her journal announcement.

"So, I want you to write about that influential moment that made you into the person you are today." The enthusiasm in her voice might have been contagious for her quartet of appeasers, but Nell remained unconvinced.

Why? Why was she so pressed to know my business?

Nell chanced a look around the room again. The squad (cheerleaders and assorted athletes) was huddled in the center desks of the classroom whispering. Jay was picking at his cuticles, brows wrinkled in concentration.

She heard the soft tapping from the new guy drumming his pen against the desktop. His twisted hair bounced as he rocked his head in time to his beat. He seemed to be mouthing something silently.

"Save it for band, Tru." Ms. Yashar's shrill voice sounded from her desk where she had settled. Ignoring the conversations of nearly every other student, she didn't even look up from her screen to single him out.

How did she even know it was him? Nell couldn't decide if he deserved the call out. It was routine now for Ms. Yashar to reserve her most passionate scolds for him. And while Tru had been the class comic relief more than once, Ms. Yashar liked to incite his performances.

She announced every missed post on the discussion board – almost happily reporting it to the class. She insulted him, mercilessly attacking him. And her insults could be brutal. Just the other day, she'd announced to the class:

"It seems Mr. Pitre doesn't want to participate in our course – though he does enough to call attention to himself here. Your name may mean clown, but this classroom is not your circus."

Her frustration was sourced from his mere presence and he irritated her consistently each block.

This time, though, Tru immediately stilled his fingers and Nell was sure she saw a flicker of sadness on his face. He didn't reply, he just picked up his pen and allowed it to click against his thumbnail long enough for Ms. Yashar to *humph* and suck her teeth. His shoulders drooped, but the noise stopped, and he started writing something.

Nell sketched a red target in her notebook. Then she sat staring at her page trying not to think about the assignment. The target blurred, a tear dropping onto the page and bleeding the ink. She closed her eyes.

The endless conversations around her peaked as the journal time dragged to a close. Parts of the inane conversations invaded her thoughts:

"You know, her stylist is gay. He's so fashionable without even trying."

"I need a gay-boy girlfriend – you know, a *'gurrrl-fren'* – someone to go shopping with who knows all the latest trends before they're trending."

"Totally. That's the kind of girlfriend every squad needs."

"We should find one."

Nell tried to ignore the disgusting conversation but she heard it clearly. She had several clever responses but didn't bother to say them. What would be the point in engaging in their ignorance, anyway?

Reading time followed, and Nell brought extra reading material to busy herself while the class collectively crawled through even the shortest excerpts. It made for a lot of extra time to do other things. Anything except think – having time for that was dangerous because her thoughts always drifted to vibrant, exuberant Aidan. He was full of life, and he loved love. A flair of flamboyance and experimental style, he dressed to impress (and encouraged Nell to borrow from his closet's wide selection of skirts, scarves and heels, often).

"Discussion group leaders?" Ms. Yashar stood in front of the white board, papers clutched to her chest. She waited for her students to acknowledge her. "Come get your focus points."

Desks scrapped the floor as they pushed them into clusters. The leaders obediently stood and took their handouts from Ms. Yashar.

Nell waited, watching the groups form around her. Brody grabbed her desk, placing it next to the four others of their assigned group.

"Le'go," he said impatiently, shoving his glasses into place on his nose. He'd fulfilled his obligation to "be inclusive;" Nell had to make an effort to reciprocate.

She stood, holding her stomach muscles taut, and adjusted the fall of her shirt, acutely aware that she'd made herself conspicuous by lingering in her row. Dragging her chair behind her, she joined her desk and the group, and quickly sat.

"Shelly's party is in two weeks. Did you get an invite?" Claire, still making plans to fill her social calendar, spoke past Nell to someone in another group. She rolled sparkled gloss across her lips and rubbed them together, noticing that she'd caught the admiring eyes of several guys.

"Uh... this says to discuss the restrictions of Samsa now that he is transformed and how these physical issues affect his mental prowess. What the ... what?" Alex waved the assignment paper at Brody. He had no idea what the novella was about, probably hadn't even tried to read it.

"Hmm... she wants to know if being an insect alters — that means changes — Gregor Samsa's smarts." Brody translated. "Since no one cares he's a creature, and it's just his body that isn't human, it doesn't. Yashar's probably checking to see if we read the story."

"Well *I* didn't," Claire shrugged. She was looking at something on her phone. "He's now a bug. So what?"

Nell, who did read the novella, slumped in her chair, eyes downcast.

"Really Claire?" Brody adjusted his glasses.

She shooed him with a wave of her hand while still staring at her phone. "I have a life." And with that, she put them – and the discussion – on disregard.

"You're up, Nell."

Spotlight. She hated these group discussions. She had to participate, though, as Ms. Yashar might decide to look up from her computer or, worse, walk around checking groups. Involvement was mandatory even if the contribution sucked.

She began, "His intelligence isn't an issue except that he can't communicate with the people he loves. His new... appearance sickens his family. He's... rejected. His identity is trapped in a foreign body. He... He didn't choose his fate but they *chose* to get rid of him."

She felt the stares of students in other groups. *Shit. Too loud. Is everything going to remind me of him?* This discussion was about Samsa – a Kafka character, not her brother. Aidan was dead. Her big brother died just before the school year started. And Nell blamed their father's rejection for killing him.

The timer on Ms. Yashar's desk signaled the end of the session. This time, Nell was first to move back to her row.

"Awesome discussions today," Ms. Yashar said. She'd moved to stand in front of the white board and was pointing to a date on the paper calendar she held. "This is posted online, of course, but I want to remind you that you'll be choosing your partners for the PSA performance projects. I've booked the auditorium for you to present three weeks from now."

Nell felt queasy. Her face flushed, coloring her tan skin in rosy hues. Head bowed, her wavy hair fell forward, obscuring her expression. She shifted uncomfortably in the hard-plastic chair. Placing an origami bird to hold the page in her moleskin (it was far more interesting than the attached braided cord for that purpose), then carefully arranging the book in her schoolbag, she resolved to avoid the next class by any excuse she could find.

Tru

I don't know what it is about that girl. The whole class is a mess and she sits there on the outskirts with her head bowed low. The girls talk through her but she doesn't notice. Or maybe she don't care? My guess is she wants invisibility.

Nell. I think that's what Teach called her. She's one of the first to arrive and last to leave, without so much as a nod at her from anyone. That's not normal when e'ry seat in the room is filled.

I'm hella sure she aint looking for friends, but I... I'm guessing she needs one. And my gut tells me she's more than just a little lonely. You don't have to advertise for attention to wish someone acknowledged your existence. I know.

I get lots of attention for all the wrong reasons – my height, my melanin, my manhood. But in this class – in this school – I was supposed to get a new start. There's no playground crew to call me out on myself, so I can be Tru without a record, without a past. The rebirth began day one and I'm making sure that out here, Tru is synonymous with comic genius.

But Nell? She must have one hell of a story and I want to read it.

Every class, she's busy *avoiding* the class.

Stealing a look her way is dangerous. I could spend some time counting her explosion of freckles. Or watching the tears she can't control slide down her cheeks. I'm intrigued. She's... different.

As it is, I see her slumped over that sketchbook daily with her pen moving feverishly over the once-blank pages. One time my curiosity got the best of me, so I passed her desk like I was sharpening my pencil just to steal a glance. She has mad skills. The page was covered in this elaborate portrait of some guy dressed in... I dunno, drag or something. His pose looked GQ – like something out of *Gentleman's Quarterly* – but he had on a skirt that wasn't matching the dark scruffy beard, suit jacket, and slender tie. I didn't look long 'cause I know she felt me pass by and she don't know me. I aint one to jump in nobody's business uninvited.

I'll ask Zeke. He seems to know everyone as one of the many pseudo-celebrities of Ms. Yashar's class. Where I'm from, soccer players aren't exactly top of the street cred rosters, but every jock and cheerleader in this joint seems to rank high up on the same popularity chart. Zeke hasn't let it get to his head though. He's an ai'ight guy and seems genuine. Actually, so far the sports athletes have all been cool, but the Pom Pom Posse? Nah. Each one of them needs to be handled with care or avoided entirely. Take Carrie. She reminds me of the female in *Cruel Intentions*, and I aint trying to get into her sights because she's dangerous. Cheerleading here is cutthroat, I guess.

I waited a few days to ask. "You want to know about Nell? All these lovies in here and you're asking about her?" Zeke actually thought I was feeling the girl. This wasn't a romantic inquiry.

"It aint like that, man. I'm curious. She's... a curiosity. You gotta see that?"

He smirked at me and shook his head, but I know he *knew* what I meant.

Even so, I went on. "Head bowed down into that book of hers. She gives that moleskin mad love and ignores life around her. What's her deal?"

"Can't say for certain. Nell's not a talker. Never was the befriending type. But when her big bro died last summer, it's like she went with him. Shame. She could be a looker and she's smart as hell." His wrist phone vibrated then, and he glanced at the message. "Hmmm, Kaycee. Gotta take this." Shrugging, he walked away.

If I asked anyone else, the rumor mill would report that I was crushing on the poor girl. She didn't need that kind of attention. And while I really don't care what these folk think, I prefer being the enigma.

Isn't that a great word? Enigma. A mystery. A question. Pitre, the clown of unknown origin (though my name is French from my Creole kin).

I get it. Nell is an enigma, too. She doesn't want attention and doesn't need these people to care. But I'm intrigued - - hella interested in knowing more about her and I don't know why.

***

Here I am fixated on this girl, and my report card is in jeopardy. At this point, Ms. Yashar isn't accepting anything I turn in on paper and my grade is plummeting. I'm starting to think it's a straight waste of time to try. I've never been in a class where the teacher was so adamant about sticking to her syllabus that she refused to consider her students as individuals. Granted I didn't tell her about my court situation – that I'm restricted from all internet accessible devices from using a computer to my smart phone. How could I confide in her? She'd probably want to confirm my story. One call from her to my college, and they might revoke my acceptance. I can't risk it. If she doesn't grade my work soon, though, it won't matter anyway. My final transcript needs to be on point.

So I do the work the only way I can. Zeke's been great about printing out the assignments or he dictates them to me when I call from the phone in our apartment. When I turned in the first handwritten assignment, Teach balked at it. My cursive is legible, it's even been praised before, but she acted like she couldn't decipher a single word on the page.

So I bought a typewriter – a great find at the thrift store with extra ribbons and paper sold as part of the package. I type up the next assignment and the one after it. Still, she scoffed at me when I turned over the papers.

I saw her set all my work on the corner of her desk in a pile. She didn't read any of it – I'm certain of that, because the printed progress report she sent home at midterm was a clear F.

How can she call herself an educator and be so unreasonably rigid?

***

Tonight, my pen's been busy. I write when I'm thinking. Or stressin'. But right now? I'm tired – fed up with my situation.

I don't know Ms. Yashar's background. She's jai like prejudice, but I still aint 100 on whether it's about me being Black or poor or something else she saw in me that struck her foul even before I began my classroom production.

Teach

You taught me
The lesson?
Every crayon in this box –
  Aint equal
Colors gotta stay in line
All but one
  Encouraged to go outside
  And over
Changing those beneath
  To a preferred hue
No longer vibrant

Diluted to blend better
On the page.

Nell

She sat on the dark hardwood floor of the newly established guest room that once belonged to Aidan.

The decor was stiff and foreign: a mahogany dresser, a large frame bed with starched smooth beige sheets and grey comforter. No photographs, no color. The window was covered in slated mahogany blinds - a perfect match to the furniture. The stale air was choking, and the stark white light cast harsh illumination over the space.

It was times like these when her father just didn't understand; yet another moment in her life that she had to seek solace from his intolerance. With Aidan gone, there was no one she could talk to about her troubles, about anything personal really, but she could at least go to his room and feel some sense of comfort.

When he was alive, she'd often times rap on his door and wait anxiously for him to answer with cheery face and open arms. He would welcome her, plopping her down onto his big bed with the ultra-soft purple Sherpa blanket and ask her what was going on. There they'd sit for hours with crisscrossed legs or lay side by side staring up at the ceiling with legs dangling off the edge and folded arms supporting their heads.

He didn't mind that this was his little sister. Whether just shooting the breeze as though they were longtime best friends or taking on her nightmares, Big Brother never treated her like an outsider in his space, or an intruder to his peace.

If she closed her eyes now, she could feel his presence. It was a relationship that she treasured and one she desperately missed.

One time just before he moved out, he invited her to try a black charcoal mask. The two smoothed on the tar like substance, feeling it pull taught as it dried. They danced, then. Mimicking "The Mask" as they sashayed a salsa and sang "They call me Cuban Pete... boom chicka boom... boom chicka boom..."

Then, it was time to tear it off, and Aidan volunteered to go first. Nell peeled back a side slowly as he grimaced, gripping the dresser in agony.

"Wow." He said it through clenched teeth. "Just... do it." And she yanked the stubborn black goo as he squelched a whine. Aidan refused to torture Nell that way, so he soaked her mask off with warm wash cloths.

"Girl. The scathing product review I'm gonna write for this..."

Reminders of Aidan continued to come into her head day in and day out at the most inopportune times rendering her powerless against raw sorrow.

She had felt the building tension of her father's rage against his son.

First, he condemned Aidan's fashion, which often seemed lifted from the edgy advertisements of Louis Vuitton or, sometimes, borrowed from *The Fifth Element*'s Ruby Rhod. When Aidan came home from his college lecture holding a satchel etched in flowers, his father guffawed and his eyes bulged as he stared at the offense. Aidan's plaid skirt, which he wore with a suit jacket, collared shirt and tie sent Mr. Necahual into a choking fit and he spit out his tea. Even Aidan's boat shoes and skinny slacks were challenged.

Despite the resistance, Aidan was a free spirit. Mr. Necahual prided himself on machismo – on showcasing his masculinity and strength with an almost disgusting tenacity. And his son seemed determined to do the opposite. Nothing he said dimmed Aidan's shine.

Then Aidan found love with Charles, and darkness fell.

Chay, as he preferred to be called, was a man their father neither accepted or respected. He was forbidden to cross the threshold of their home.

"No son of mine…" He chastised Aidan. "Never would I imagine. Queers are not in *my* family."

"Dad. Are you serious? I'm gay, not queer." Aidan laughed nervously, cleared his throat, and continued in his deep voice that trembled ever-so-slightly as he confronted his father. "Aunt Earline is the weird one. I'm unique - eccentric, perhaps - and I'm asking you please, let me bring Charles with me to Thanksgiving dinner. You will *love* him."

Aidan smirked at his joke, knowing his father was not amused and would never understand the punchline.

"You... you... you'll burn in hell. Not in my house. No. He is not welcome here. *You* are not welcome here." Mr. Necahual was not a religious man, so this outburst made little sense.

"Wait. Dad?"

"Don't *you* call me that."

Nell listened from the hallway as her father's voice rose. He was seething. *Please, Dad. Don't push him away. Aidan isn't doing anything wrong. He's in love and he is…* As she thought back to that last argument, she remembered even the most minute details. Her father's booming voice spewing hellfire at his only son. Her brother's deep voice awkwardly crackling and uncertain as he pleaded for himself – for everything that made Aidan who he was. And the moment he gave in and gave up on the family.

The house shook as the front door slammed. She rushed into the living room, pulled back the curtain, and saw Aidan's car speed away. He never entered their house again.

For several weeks after Aidan left, Nell would sneak out of her house to visit him. Disappearing for hours at a time under the guise of going to the library to complete something for studies, she'd bike around the corner to the small rented studio Aidan shared with Chay. Sometimes he wasn't home when she arrived, but she couldn't call ahead because her father paid the phone bill and he checked the numbers incoming and outgoing. Turning her phone off, she'd wait for one of them to arrive, sitting on the homeowner's porch swing quietly fearing that the landlord might chase her away or, worse, that her father might drive down the street looking for her.

Winter made it difficult to bike even the short distance to Aidan's home from her own. She couldn't risk the drive there because she'd risk her father seeing her car parked along the curb or track her vehicle, as he sometimes did.

Then Aidan was ill.

"It's just a little cold," he insisted. But weeks of coughing turned to months of progressively worse illness. Years of inhaling darkroom chemicals for hours on end must've complicated his recovery. Worried as she was, Nell's visits were cut off by increasing inquiries from their father and mother.

She'd come in from a visit, her backpack hanging over one shoulder and several notebooks in hand. Her mother met her at the door with the same stream of questions:

"Do you know what time it is? Where have you been? Surely you didn't need all that time to study? What class is all this for?"

There were no pauses for responses, as she didn't want to hear the explanation.

Why do you even bother, Mom.? You didn't worry about Aidan walking out that door never to return. Do you know he is dying?

Effectively abandoned, Aidan died alone, save for his boyfriend of several years. He died in a converted garage apartment several blocks away from the family home. Their father didn't call Aidan when the doctor said this would likely be his last week — there was nothing more to do except make him comfortable. He didn't come to his bedside when they said Aidan was at the end — as Aidan labored to breathe and winced in pain. Mr. Necahual wasn't there to hear him say his last words, "tell Dad I forgive him."

I wasn't there either. In fact, she was on lockdown — closely monitored by an increasingly suspicious father and a mother who feared repercussions if she made exceptions to her husband's family rules.

Chay later told her about those final moments reluctantly. She had insisted he hold back nothing. After some prodding, he produced a letter for her, penned in Aidan's immaculate, slanted script.

"He left this for you, Nell, with apologies that it might be a bit messy."

It was a short letter.

> "Nell-Belle, my *fabulous* sister. The doctor says I don't have much longer to fight. I'm going to be free to catwalk across the clouds — how does that sound? Baby girl, be amazing. You have brought me joy — you are joy. Promise me something, okay? Live loud. I want you to know that Chay and I were married (you'll have to have him show you the pictures sometime. And when I'm gone, you know you still have a big brother. I know he'll be here for you just like I am.
>
> Love ya, toots. A—"

She treasured that letter, which she kept hidden under her mattress.

Now, sitting in this sterilized space that once was home to a colorful personality, she felt numb.

"Aidan, I'm sorry," she said to the emptiness around her. "I miss you so much. You'd know exactly how to handle this stupid senior project."

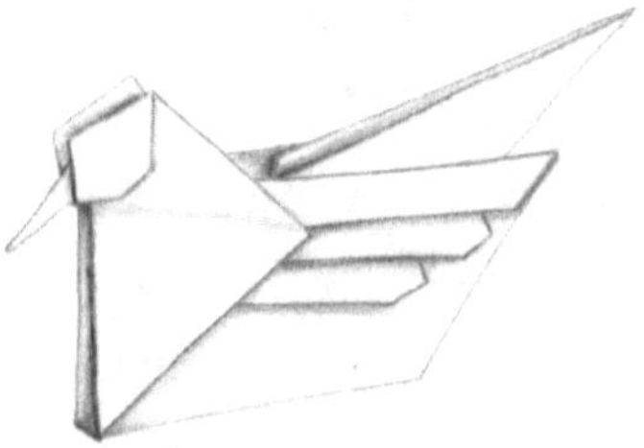

Tru

The subway always calms my nerves. The steady rumble of the tracks below my feet as I stand — by choice — for the 30 minutes it takes to cross town. I watch the intermittent lights from passing lamp posts. Gripping the hand strap, my pulse is intensified against the rubber. Behind me, other passengers follow the commuters' rule: mind your business and avoid involvement with others. The cacophony of musical genres escapes headphones and a mother tries to soothe her fussy child.

When my phone wasn't on lock, I'd play a game or a tune, but that's not possible now. No phones. And no PC, tablet, laptop, or anything else with connections. So I'm here looking through the smudges of fingerprints at the city passing me by, biding my time and minding my own. Sometimes I wear my headphones, sliding the cords into my hoodie and pretending I can't hear the happenings around me.

Jingle comes through on schedule, his ratty cargos carrying the city dirt, paint and sludge. A tangled beard clings to his neck and chin, meets up with a mustache so unkempt it covers his dark upper lip. His eyes are wild, darting from passenger to passenger seeking a compassionate face as he shuffles along and shakes his coin cup — a small, stained McCafe —

as though willing someone to add a little more sound to his clinking change. His fingernails are brown with grime, hands are gnarled with age and arthritis.

I aint got much in my pockets – a few bucks and some coin to re-up on tokens – but Jingles means no harm and I can spare a quarter for his collection.

"Bless," he says, flashing a near-toothless smile and then turning toward an elderly woman. She cowers away ostentatiously and holds a single finger sideways under her nose so it covers both nostrils as she grimaces and casts a glaring look of distain at Jingles. Then she shoots evil eyes at me for contributing.

"Encouraging the *trash*," she chastises once Jingle had shuffled far enough away to pose no presumed threat. She was still muttering when the train stopped, and I shifted temporarily to open the passage-way for several people to enter and exit.

I didn't pay her any mind. It seems like folk are always passing judgment on me and my actions. Have been all my life.

The subway car door closes and I move to stand in front of it again. I can see the passengers through the cloudy glass, but I look like I'm checking my own reflection. The scold is holding her purse tightly against her. Her seat neighbor – a man in a suit with a newspaper on his lap and cell in hand – doesn't notice her discomfort. Old biddy scared of everyone, that's tough when you're relegated to public transit.

It takes me nearly an hour to get into the city. From the train, I take the four blocks to the rec by foot. Neighborhood never changes. Little kids sit on stoops with their noses running, watching the older ones enviously as they ride bikes with mix and match parts – some with the seats raised high because the bikes are too short for their riders. Bikers pop curbs, spin, dodge the speeding cars between speed bumps. There's a hidden hustle on e'ry corner, even more in the cuts between buildings. Street pharmacy is steady money.

"Just in time, Tru. Busy schedule," Mama Vee says from behind the sign in desk. She's leaning her chest on the surface and it's hard not to double take. She waves me toward her, pulls me into her soft body for a hug, and I rest my head on her silver locs. I'm instantly relaxed into her familiarity. She pulls back to give me a once-over. Then she's shaking me – her grip firm on my shoulders – as she throws her head back in a chuckle from the depths of her soul. "I didn't think you'd be back here now that you and Steph are in suburbia. How's it treating you, chile?"

Mama Vee has known me from the cradle. I'm pretty sure she's known Ma from diapers, too. She's a constant here and she takes care of her "kids" even though her own is gone. "I couldn't save him from the streets," she told me once, "Im'ma make damn sure none of you ever get in 'em." She was at my trial, rocking herself on the wooden courtroom bench like it was a pew and the stenographer was playing the church organs. Mama Vee tugged on my lawyer's suit jacket when the judge began rattling off my punishments – she volunteered to supervise my community service.

"You know, Mama Vee. Gotta keep ya head up. Won't get me caught up... graduation is just around the corner. Like 'Pac said, 'You either evolve or you disappear,' and I'm here for all to see."

"I knew it, baby. My Tru cannot fail... even when you falter." Man, Mama Vee's smile lights up the world. Next to Ma, no one has more confidence in me – not even *me*.

Nell

Her mother wasn't expected to be home before nightfall and her father was surveying a new property his company was contracted to build on. It was still early, so Nell set off on her bicycle.

She had no real destination in mind, just wanted to escape the cold sterility of her parents' house. It didn't feel like home to her and she felt robbed of oxygen when she stayed inside. Her father and mother monitored her comings and goings closely (electronic trackers left little opportunity for going off the grid). They also periodically searched her room – Nell caught her mother in her dresser drawers and closet on more than one occasion "just straightening the clothes, darling, and putting these few things from the cleaners where they belong. You don't mind do you?"

She *did* mind. And knowing there was no private space she could claim in the house, Nell always kept her satchel with her.

As she peddled down the street, wind whipping against her face, she found herself drawn to Aidan and Chay's home. Chay's car was parked on the curb and the driveway was empty. Nell walked her bike up the drive, and carefully rested the bike against the garage before wrapping four times on the side door – the magic number, Aidan had said.

"Who is it?" Chay's voice sounded muffled from behind the door.

"It's Nell, brother dear."

She heard several latches click and moments later, Chay was ushering her into the house.

"Nell-Belle! I wasn't expecting you. Oh the mess," he said as he straightened photo albums into stacks of three on his coffee table that served dual function as the dinner table in the tiny space. The home was immaculate, as always.

"I'm sorry, I…"

"Nonsense. Never apologize, little sis." His smile was infectious. "Mi casa es su casa and all that jazz." His laugh, sudden and loud, reverberated against the walls.

"I'm glad someone's home is. Mine certainly isn't."

"Aww, Nell-Belle. What's going on now?"

"Same as always. Andreas must have perfection – wife, house, daughter. You know what happens when something, no, some*one* doesn't measure up. And Lia? In her world, imperfections are simply ignored if she can't fix them. *I* am her latest irreparable failure."

"You, my dearest, could never be a failure. Where's that moleskin of yours? What have you been working on since our last tête-à-tête?"

"Our wha--- Oh, you've been working with the stone again, huh?"

"Sim, sim. Rosetta Stone is wonderous. I'm studying French, Spanish, and Portuguese. I thought about adding Latin to this romance of mine, but that, my love, is dead."

"Chay, you amaze me."

"I amaze myself, dah-ling. As our Aidan liked to say, 'Perfection is over-rated, but my rating is extraordinary!'"

"That you are," she smiled and nodded. "Just a few new additions in the sketchbook. I've been trying out new pencils."

"Have you thought about watercolors? The blends are divine – though I see you've got a few blurs going on in some of this pen work." He flipped the book towards her, tapping a tear stained page.

Nell shrugged. There was no reason to explain the obvious. Chay knew. She wasn't coping well, he'd told her. *Aidan would've said to live it up double for him.* But that was not in Nell's character.

She reached toward one of the photo albums, but Chay swatted playfully at her hand. He picked a book from the stack and handed it to her. "This one is my favorite of his work," he said.

Minutes rolled into hours, with Nell and Chay reminiscing about Aidan over his photographs. "Oh, no. It's getting late. I've got to beat Lia home," Nell said, checking her watch.

"Do you need a ride home, kiddo?"

"No, I have my bike."

He pulled her into a hug and she inhaled the familiar scent of cologne. "Is that?"

"Yeah. I missed it, so I picked some up."

"Oh."

On the way back home, she felt her spirits lift. Chay was the love of Aidan's life. He supported his photography and shared his dreams. He and Aidan made plans for their future. And now, even with Aidan gone, he welcomed Nell into his life and comforted her as she mourned their mutual loss.

As she turned onto her street, she frowned. She'd stayed out too long and her mother was home – she knew from the lights in the den. *Brace yourself.*

She closed the door behind her as softly as she could but as it clicked shut, she heard movement. She could feel her mother's proximity.

"I'm home!" Surely, if she pre-empted the confrontation, it would lessen the severity.

"You should never have left," her mother's voice was full of unwarranted aggravation. "Where have you been?"

"At the library, mom." Nell tried to keep her tone level, respectful. She wasn't in the mood for this tonight.

Luckily, her mother did not move to confront her further as she padded down the hall in her socks. Nell closed her bedroom door, pushing the lock in to ensure no surprise invasions. *Times like these...* retrieving her sketchbook from her satchel, she lay on her bed and started to draw. It was a good thing senior year was moving so quickly.

Tru

"Answer for roll," Ms. Yashar starts up right as the bell stops. She rattles off the list of students from her roster without glancing up at any of us.

***

Sometimes I don't get her. She's disliked me at first sight and seems to be trying to make the feeling mutual. I aint got love for her, but I don't have nothin' against her either. Teach got issues. I know her but she don't think I do. She sure as hell don't know me.

Class drags. Ms. Yashar thinks of herself as someone shaping the future of the world. Today she is trying to inspire us with some life lessons. She starts with the usual activities – on a notecard write three goals then flip it over and write the steps needed to accomplish 'em.

I'm staring at this card for a good minute. It came from a multicolor pack of 5x7 cards; I usually don't see any of 'em that aren't white and 4x6, not that it matters or anything. But she handed me this obnoxiously green card from her stack and all I can do is inspect it.

"It's a notecard, Tru. You have instructions," she says it before half the class even got their cards as though I am holding up her flow.

I debate for a bit about what goals to write on that florescent paper. My goals?

1. Graduate from this replacement school without incident
2. Settle my court issues and see the judge wipe my record clean
3. Make movies in the N-Y-C

I have all the steps and the plan is in action. But I can't write any of that on this card. I start to write something several times but erase it.

"Don't you sweep that trash on the floor," Yashar has stopped mid exchange of notecards to direct me.

"Ma'am? Are you serious?" I say it before I can catch myself.

"Most certainly. The trashcan is next to you. I don't know how you behave in your home, but here we are respectful of our custodians."

She *is* serious. And she managed to disrespect me as she calls me out. Her eyes pierce into mine as she wills me to comply. Eraser bits aren't exactly worth the effort of gathering up and carrying to the can. Fo'real, she is trippin' but I have no choice but to acknowledge the absurd command.

Pom Pom Posse and several others snicker as I sweep the residual eraser into my hand with the card and obediently drop the offensive pink waste into the can.

"It's a wonder you haven't snapped back at her yet," Zeke leans forward to whisper at me.

"Can't. That's not my vibe. I much prefer a little comedy to liven my mood." I tip my imaginary hat and do a one-man wave from one arm to the other from my seat.

What was I gonna put on this card?

I settle on jotting down two truths and a lie, hoping Ms. Yashar is up for a bit of a challenge.

In my neatest handwriting, I write:

1.   Attend school for cinematic directing, screenwriting and filmmaking

2.   Create a touring stand-up comedy and variety show

3.   Write urban fiction

Writing the flip side was easy. My steps? Graduate. Relocate. *Carpe diem* — seize the day; although it more accurately means focus on the now and forget about later, which kinda negates the whole steps to accomplish my goals idea.

I finish the task with time to spare. Honestly, I can't imagine why it took anyone longer than a few seconds to jot down their futures, but as I scan the room, quite a few of my classmates are struggling.

On the far side of the room, a kid named Larry is chewing on his eraser. Teach should be on *his* case. He's wasting a perfectly good eraser he knows he can't digest. She doesn't even notice him. She's back at her desk looking at her computer screen while an egg timer she's set to 10 minutes clicks away.

"What'd you put on your card, Claire?"

"You know. Daddy's sending me on an after-graduation vay-kay. After that, who cares? Maybe school."

"For your M. R. S. degree?"

"Of course!"

An M. R. S. — *Missus*, not a Bachelor's. The tragedy is she's going to waste her father's generosity by husband shopping on some campus.

Finally, the timer dings its bell and Yashar stands. She click clacks in those high heels she wears to the center front of the room with a big smile. "Dreams with a plan in place are goals, not fantasies. Let's hear what you all have in store in the coming years." Scanning the room of students — most of whom are attempting to avoid making eye contact, their heads slightly bowed and eyes downcast, she picks her target.

Monica is on her phone and Zeke is on his, the tell-tale glow from their laps giving it away. The two are probably texting each other. Ol' school notes aren't a thing in this school, 'cause e'rybody got a celly. But back home, she'd have put pen to paper and then passed her intricately and carefully folded love note across the rows to him. That's the kind of in-class talking I prefer. I can savor a note well after the moment's passed – can't do that with a text. Phone messages have no personality, no care, no scent of the sender attached. Jo and I, though we aint never been a couple, only sent texts at night when the urgency of the message couldn't wait until we passed through the halls and could slip a note to one another.

Teach settles her scope on Nell, who is sitting cross-legged in her chair, pen to moleskin, entranced in her own creativity.

"Nell, what is one goal you've set?"

She starts from the sudden spotlight of attention. "I… uh, to move away from here."

"For what purpose?" Ms. Yashar counters quickly. "And where to?"

"To find contentment; and, anywhere but here," she answers with a finality as if daring further inquiry.

"Well then," she's nodding, clearly rattled by the retort. "Anthony?"

"Yeah?"

"Your goal."

"Oh yeah. I'm going to travel a bit after I graduate. Then in the fall, I'm off to college on my track and field scholarship."

"How nice, Anthony, congratulations!"

"That's what's up," Zeke adds, shaking his fist in the air as a sort of 'right on.'

She calls a few other students, nodding happily and offering encouragement to each, then she turns abruptly to me.

"And you, Tru? What is your goal if you graduate," she says – just like that, *if.*

I mean, what the hell? Of course I'm gonna graduate.

"Ms. Yashar, I have several goals," I start, and she interjects.

"And they are?" Her impatience with me is painful.

"I'm going to college, Ms. Yashar. My future in cinematography starts there."

"I see." She doesn't inquire further. Instead, she moves on with our agenda. "Okay. In just a few minutes, I'll take the first choices for partners for the PSA project. And before you even ask, no one is working alone. Collaboration is key." She sang that last line with a bit of sass and I'm thinking that the department is pushing some initiative she's not too fond of following.

I've never seen such a swift reaction to a group assignment. E'rybody in the class was talking at once, with the Pom Pom Posse quickly pairing up as they scanned the room with disdain for the less desirable partners. Carrie pointed and spoke to Sue from behind her hand to muffle her words as both girls chuckled mercilessly.

A teacher I once had loved to use the word "scoff," as in "don't scoff at him, there is nothing funny about his answer." That's exactly what the girls' laughter reminded me of — always laughing at someone's expense without remorse. No one wanted to be their punchline.

Some of these jokers remind me of the soldiers in that movie "Renaissance Man" - the Double-Ds, who clearly needed some help with academic basics. They live for group work to salvage their grades as the designated brains do the assignment and they claim credit for participation. I'm laughing at them as they eagerly stake claim of less than fervent classmates too timid to decline the partnership.

There must be some strategy to picking a partner in this high-stake assignment. I expected the cliques to do their thing, mocking the fringe while linking up. They did not disappoint.

I worry about that Nell, though. She hasn't uttered a word beyond the required during our "analytic response group discussions." I've been in this class going on a month and she's jai like mute. No polite, obligatory "hello," no "hey there, how ya doin'." She walks these halls with her head bowed down, watching her feet and feeling out her path without catching anyone's eyes. Nobody bothers her, don't even seem like they know she's here. There are no secrets shared with friends, no casual exchanges. She don't even have a rapport with Teach (though honestly, Ms. Yashar aint exactly the most welcoming toward human interaction. She's straight up distant and often distracted.)

Nell seems to only have refuge when she's working in that moleskin. And from the looks of her work — I'd stolen a few more viewings in passing — she pours her hurt onto every page.

She's sitting in her usual spot, huddled over the open book with a… is that a jar of ink and a quill? Serious. Her hair is spilling over most of her face, but what I can see is strangely pale like she's lost her color from fear. Stressing this pair-up, I'm certain. Damn, I don't need another project. The last one got me caught up terrible and I'm still paying my "debt to society."

But then… maybe I can help us both with this assignment. I don't need new connects here and she clearly wants no attachments.

Teach finishes her roll - and whatever paperwork teachers do - stretching out the process to give us time to figure it out. She moves to the center of the room with a clipboard. Then, dramatically stretching her arms out like she's summoning God or something, she says, "Let the partnerships commence!"

I'm guessing she's done this move before because no one even snickers at her. Instead, several students crowd around her declaring their duos as though someone would fight to take someone's claim.

Zeke comes up to my desk, a weird look on his face as he approaches. "So are you going to go solo on this project?"

"Naw man. Not testin' her wrath. Just waiting for the crowd to die down."

"I'm'a use this project for time with my girl. Mo and I, man… Ms. Yashar has some timing."

"Unh. Well, you know me. I get it done. Teach aint gonna be happy with my effort no way."

He nods. There isn't a kid in this class who thinks the teacher appreciates me. "Man. You rub her in all the wrong ways. Man." He walks away, draping his arm around Monica's waist and pulling her close.

By this point, most of the students are lingering around the classroom in the usual groups. I check the clock. One minute to dismissal. It's perfect. I stand up slowly and make my way the short distance to Ms. Yashar. She's talking with one of her favorites, Lillian, who rattles off the perfect answer for every in-class question. Both of them ignore my approach.

"Ms. Yasha- -" I'm drowned out by the bell ringing. The class leaves in a jumble, tossing bags over shoulders and sliding notebooks into secure places against their chests. I remind myself again that the 'burbs prides itself on conformity as I note the number of designer labels on those school supplies.

Teach watches as her class files out - including Lillian with her two long braids bouncing behind her. Then Yashar walks back to her cluttered desk. I'm determined, so I follow her and try to be nonchalant as I block her in by standing in the small opening between her desk and the wall. She sees me and sighs.

I survey the empty class – except for Nell, who is still looking a bit pale. She's meticulously straightening her sketching supplies, then closes a... is that origami? into her moleskin to hold her place. Damn, girl, *go*.

Ms. Yashar looks a bit confused as I stand here, but she doesn't rush me to state my business. Finally, Nell skulks from the classroom silently.

"Poor girl," Teach shakes her head as her gaze follows Nell. "She never was a social one, but now---" I suspect she might have said more, but it's then that she realizes it's me who can hear her.

"Ms. Yashar, she's exactly why I need to talk to you."
"What?"

"Nell. I'd like to partner with her on the PSA project… that is if she doesn't already have one?"

"Huh." She sort of laughs, sort of snorts the reply. " Why would I…" she continues, but doesn't finish uttering the thought.

"I assume she isn't spoken for?" Teach is looking at me like I'm not speaking in English anymore.

"You want to work with Nell? You…"

"Yes, ma'am. You said we have to collaborate. I don't have a partner. I don't think she does, either. I'm volunteering to pair up."

"Does Nell know your intentions?"

"My intentions?" I know she doesn't think I'm'a do the assignment. She thinks I'm a consummate slacker – that I'm stupid. Fair enough, I've not given her any reason to suspect otherwise if you only consider the digiclass, but my work on paper shoulda been evidence enough that I'm no dummy. I can't trust her, so I'm not offering her the story. "I just think she needs a partner and no one speaks to her, really. But if you do pair us, don't tell her I offered. Please."

"I don't think… Tru?"

"Ma'am, I mean no harm." She looks at me straight, scrutinizes my face until I'm kinda uncomfortable with the attention. "I don't want her to think…" I pause to gather my thoughts as I start to stammer. "Just maybe ask her to pair up with the partnerless clown?"

"Okay. I suppose I can assign you to work with her, though I have real reservations."

"Thank you." I don't give her a chance to expound on her concerns or change her mind. Just spin around, grab my pack, and rush off to second block.

Nell

Nell was determined not to return to Ms. Yashar's class the next morning. However, she was not the kind of student to play hooky, binging on movies or reading in bed while pretending to nurse a sore throat or other ailment. Never the convincing fibber – because she never really lied – she just couldn't pull off a sick day unless she actually was ill. Besides, being at home meant that she might have to encounter one of her parents for longer than their mandatory family dinner hour and even that was too long to sit under scrutiny.

The alarm rang at 4:55am, as scheduled, but Nell had been awake and staring up at the glow stars Aidan had stuck to her ceiling years ago as a surprise.

"Dream under the stars," he'd told her when he walked her into the room and moved his hands from covering her eyes. He beamed as she took in the effect the green solar system had on the dark room. "Do you like it Nell-Belle?" She swung into his embrace and he held her close. "You deserve the world, baby girl. Don't settle for less," he whispered, pressing his chin against her head. She could feel his breathy words on her hair.

Nell missed those moments.

She quickly silenced the alarm, slipped out of bed, and went to her bathroom. Pulling her hair into a severe chignon bun to match her mood, she plucked her cheeks for some color, splashed water on her face, and surveyed the array of makeup her mother insisted on supplying but she refused to wear. She shrugged at herself in the mirror and made her way back to the room.

She'd laid out her clothes the night before on the hook next to her closet – the usual uniform of dark slacks, dark button-down sweater and a pale collared shirt. Inside her bottom dresser drawer, she pulled out a wooden box. Sitting on the bed, she lifted the lid and breathed in Aidan's cologne. The smell was still strong, and she'd purchased a vile of the scent and to spritz the contents should it ever fade. She fingered the silk ties inside, selecting one of his favorites to wear as a belt. Then, she gently closed the box and returned it to its place.

You can handle this project, Nell. Just get through the partnering and you'll survive the assignment.

She snatched her keys from the tray on her dresser, picked up her bag and sketch book from the artist's desk in front of her bedroom window, and made her way downstairs and out the door. When she had her car, the drive to school took 10 minutes, but she preferred to stretch out her short commute by driving toward the edge of town. The tree lined streets were quiet, even during this rushing hour, so she'd drive just below the speed limit and savor the scenery.

Sometimes, if she timed it right, she could idle in front of Chay's house for a minute or two and wait for him to head out to work. She'd smile and wave at him – dressed in his suit and carrying his briefcase to the edge of the drive where his beat-up car was parked – he'd flash a welcoming smile in return. "Nell-Belle! How are you, love?" he'd bellow in his deep voice, before sliding behind the wheel. He'd rev the engine, which sputtered in protest, and drive off with a wave. After the first time, it was a routine interaction. Soon, though, she knew he'd move out of the rented garage apartment and into a space more fitting for an up and coming attorney.

When she finally parked in the student lot at the high school, it was quarter to 7am. She stalled, organizing her dash compartment contents. Then, reluctantly, she gathered her stuff and made her way into the school and down the hallway to Ms. Yashar's classroom. Arriving seconds before the tardy bell, she slid into her seat and waited for the inevitable doling out of assignments. *Rejects and freaks who don't merit volunteer partners get the dregs.*

"Hello! It's partner pairing day two. We really must finalize our groups so you can get on this project." Ms. Yashar begins the class. "I've arranged for the top public service announcements to be aired on local TV. Imagine the exposure for all your hard work. Exciting!"

Nell slumps into her chair.

"Nell?" Ms. Yashar, waves her to her desk and waits for her to come. "I need a favor of you. It seems Tru over there needs a partner. I was hoping you might work with him."

Nell looks in the direction of Ms. Yashar's nod. Tru, the new guy — the one she calls the clown. *She cannot be serious. Is this a set up?* "Uh…"

"I think the project is pretty clear, so this shouldn't be a difficult paring. You can meet in here after school to work on the planning and research."

"If you think it would be wise…"

Tru, who had been looking intently at a book, felt the attention was on him. He rose and came over to the desk. Nell looked him over. Tall, wearing a plain tee and jeans. Curly twists in his chestnut brown hair. Stubble on his chin. *Wow, his eyes are quite green.* "'Sup Tea – Ms. Yashar? Pardon me, uh, Nell, is it?"

"Yes, Nell." She hoped she hadn't been staring. "Ms. Yashar says you don't have a partner for the PSA?"

"She's right, I don't. Are you saying you're free?"

"No." He looked a bit stunned by her terseness. *Oops.*

"Oh, I… uh…"

"I'm working with you. It's Tru, right?"

"It's true if you're cool about it." He laughed at his own joke and Nell's tension eased a bit.

"Well, okay then. Tru and Nell, you are partnered." Ms. Yashar jotted the names onto her clipboard list.

After school, Tru was already waiting for Nell in the classroom, holding an earmarked and paperclipped copy of *The Rose That Grew From Concrete*. Ms. Yashar was at her desk, staring at her computer monitor, occasionally clicking the mouse. Nell walked in and set her bags down. Neither looked at her. Tru was speaking aloud, but he seemed only to be talking to himself.

"'…they ordered extermination of all minds they couldn't control…'" he said.

Nell waited a moment, contemplating interrupting him. He shook his head, turned a few pages, and started again.

"'…I was the tree who grew from weeds and wasn't meant to be/ ashamed I'm not in fact I am proud/ of my thriving family tree.'"

"That was beautiful."

Tru started, suddenly aware of Nell's proximity. "Uh, thanks. 'Pac — It's a poem he wrote called 'Family Tree.'"

"Sometimes I think we're all weeds."

"*Hungh*. Probably are, in a way. I definitely aint what I think my Ma thought she was plantin', but I try to make her proud."

"Well… I gave up on pleasing my mother awhile ago," she thumbed her fingers across her moleskin sketchbook, watching the images on each page jump as she flipped through the sheets.

Ms. Yashar's clicks were a steady background to their small talk. She was oblivious to their discourse. *I'm not fooled. You're listening and taking notes. Selective hearing and selective response.*

Suddenly awkward as she stood a few feet from Tru, she took a desk chair and fished through her bag for a notebook and pen. "So, do you know what you want this PSA to be about?"

He runs through a few suggestions.

"No… nope… nuh uh… no."

"So what are *you* thinking then?"

"I hadn't really thought about it."

"But you aint feelin' my ideas?"

"No. If it's been done a lot, we shouldn't do a remake. Right?"

"I got you, but this aint getting us anywhere. I shoot out ideas and you're bullet proof."

"That's a metaphor I've not heard before."

"Where I'm from, bullets aren't figurative."

"Where you're from?"

"Yes."

"And where is that?"

"It sure aint here. So, you got any ideas generating yet? We better get this moving. I have an… appointment in a few." He checked the wall clock, shaking his head. It surprised her that he'd resort to analog for the time.

Nell tried to discretely search for a bulging pocket for a cell. Flat pockets, not even a wallet protruding from his jeans. *Interesting, no phone. Who doesn't have a phone? Maybe he keeps it in his bag?*

"So, Nell…?"

"I'm sorry. What about gangs? Addiction?"

"Have you ever met anyone in a gang?" He wasn't trying to be critical; she could tell by his tone. But he was clearly skeptical about her street knowledge, of which she admittedly had none.

"No," she started almost apologetically. "But there are gangs. A PSA about not joining would make sense."

"No sale. This school – this community – isn't building gang task forces. How many kids from this town you think were recruited into gangs? As for addiction, depends on the substance or habit. But I think that's gonna be the route e'ryone takes on this. We need something different. Like… suicide. When you're feeling alone, it seems like an option."

Nell cringed. She felt her face flush. Her eyes began to tear.

"Did I say something wrong?"

She didn't respond, just sat staring down into her sketchbook on her lap. Tru didn't press her, but he wondered about her sudden melancholy. Her freckled face was reddened, and he realized the bun was a new, severe hairstyle that sharpened her features and revealed wet rimmed eyes. He wondered if she were about to cry or if she was always this glassy-eyed.

"Look. I don't think we're gonna get an idea today. How about we hook up tomorrow, yeah?" Still no response. "Nell?"

"Yes. Tomorrow." She said finally, but she did not move or look up. She was thinking about him again.

"Okay." Tru brushed by her. "Later." Ms. Yashar had already stepped out of the room for something, and Nell was left by herself.

Aidan, those scabs on your wrist — you tried to end it, didn't you? Why didn't you tell me?

She inhaled deeply and forced herself to think about something else. Then, she gathered her things and walked out to her car.

She was freaking out more and more lately at the slightest things. Reminding herself that no one really knew what happened to her brother — especially not Tru who'd only just enrolled at school — she vowed to keep it together when they met for the project again.

Checking her face in the vanity mirror, she smirked. "Good thing you skipped mother's make up," she said aloud.

Tru

What the hell just happened there? I'm seriously thinking I took on more than I bargained for with Nell. I can't handle the waterworks.

She's like fine China – intriguing to look at, delicate to handle, and full of family history. I'm not sure I want to know what created the crack today, but I'm'a make damn sure I don't make it bigger.

I gotta catch myself as I ride up to the rec. Mind is wandering and keeps ending up on that map of freckles on Nell's face. Her pouty lips. Her dark hair. Wait. I am *not* falling for this girl, not at all. But she is... there's something special about her.

Mama Vee is orchestrating a youth painting class when I arrive. She's put on this smock covered in paint splatters. I'm certain she's decorated it for effect – to look like a serious, accomplished artist. Truth, she dabbles sporadically with a brush, but she's an unintentional mishmash of Picasso, Dali and Monet. Her work is interpretive.

"Ah, my Tru. I forgot you were joining us. The gym is closed for floor resurfacing, so it's acrylic masterpieces tonight. Grab a smock and canvas. It's therapeutic."

I'm a bit hesitant, but Mama Vee is smiling. "Come on, son." She flicks paint at me as I pass her where she's perched on a wooden stool. It lands on my forehead and drips into my brows. The dozen teens and several younger kids burst with laughter. Mama claps her hands playfully. "Now, let's continue. Happy buildings, happy birds, happy, happy, happy!" I realize she's mimicking Bob Ross, but this crew doesn't follow her reference.

"Mama Vee, what's the subject ya'll painting?"

"Barns."

"The bookstore?"

"No, baby. Barns. Farms – you know, Old MacDonald?"

I pull a folding chair from its perch against the wall and settle myself next to a few kids. Their canvases are full of greens and blues. Dabbing my brush into some paint I try to quickly catch up to Mama Vee's progress.

"Your barns can be any design, babies. Red or brown or something in between. Imagine it. Paint it."

Several kids pull out their cells. One in the row in front of me searches for 'images of barns.' I suddenly miss the convenience of my phone…computers... and internet access.

After the painting lesson is over, I clean up the room and return the supplies to the cabinets. By the time I'm done, it's nearly 9, so I make my way to the train for home.

***

Ma is asleep on the couch when I get to our apartment. Her smock hung from the couch back and her shoes lay just below her on the floor. I try not to rattle my keys as I step inside and will the door not to creak. I slide off my kicks and set them on the shoe mat.

Her dinner plate and silverware are on the coffee table, so I pick up her dishes and wipe down the ring left by her mug. She'd set the digital clock with its blinking neon blue digits directly above her head. In an hour, it'll bleat to announce that she should get ready for her overnight shift at the nursing home. She really must be tired to have it so close to her.

I wash the dishes and place them on the drying rack next to the sink. After taking a swig of the cran-apple juice, I wipe my mouth with my shirt sleeve and return the jug to the still-open fridge. I know, bad habit. If Ma saw me drinking out the container, she'd pop me. As I close the fridge, I study her work schedule on the door. The handwritten dates are penned in Ma's script on a scrap paper. It's held by magnets from Bolivia and Paris – places Ma dreams to travel to someday. She has a collection of these destination magnets. It looks like she's picked up a few more hours – more shifts with her increasing patient caseload. I turn off the lights in our small kitchen.

She's left the computer monitor on, and the screen casts an eerie glow around the living room. Our apartment bills are scattered around the keyboard. No matter how many overtime hours she takes, the bills pile up quicker than they can be paid. I click off the monitor and stack the notices neatly on the side of the PC box. I've made life hard, and Ma doesn't need this.

I have to be careful maneuvering about our cramped one-bedroom apartment when she is resting like this. If I wake her prematurely, she'll suffer for it later. I've already put her through enough. She's working sumthin' like 80 hours a week to cover my case costs – taking care of her patients with the same love and concern she gives me. The only reason she's home tonight is because I was doing my service hours.

"I worry. Need to know my baby is home safe," she says when I ask why she doesn't use the staff lounge and on-call rest area when she has these short-break shifts. She insists on being home when I return – even if she's knocked out from exhaustion.

Ma is my M-V-P, my most valuable person in this life. She dreams big – once for herself, and now for me. Those travel plans aren't the only thing she's sacrificed on my behalf. Looking at her now, weighed down by stress and lack of sleep, it's still obvious she is a stunning sista. Albums of her modeling photos are stacked in the top of our hall closet. I'm sure that if I hadn't come along, she'd have kept doing commercial work. Her last gig was a maternity shoot when she was carrying me – looking refreshed and excited about her prospects as she cradled her belly and smiled toward the sky.

Now, as she sleeps here, I can't resist brushing her wayward curl off her face where it'd fallen. It's risky, but I lean close to kiss her forehead and she stirs a little. "Love you ma, I'm home."

She sighs in response and I slip away into the room she's insisted I take – because I need more rest, she says. In my room, I open our shared closet to find a fresh medical uniform smock and matching pants. She'll be upset if the one she's laying in is wrinkled or frumpy even on the graveyard shift. Ma doesn't do disheveled in any way, so I know she'll want fresh gear. I hang the clean uniform outside on the hook over the bathroom door and I close myself into the room for a little privacy 'cause I gotta unwind a bit.

Popping in a VHS tape, I listen to the whir of the old machine as it winds the tape through. There's nothing like classic Chaplin shorts after a long day. Sometimes, though, I'll watch other old movies, studying the cinematography, breaking down the director's tricks, searching for editing mistakes. My VHS collection is diverse – including Spike Lee, Martin Scorsese, Hitchcock, Quentin Tarantino, Orson Wells, Elia Kazan, James Cameron, and early Tim Burton. There's nothing like a black and white from the old picture houses, but I also marvel at fresher exploratory work. I lucked up on some perfect condition tapes at the thrift.

By next year, I'll be shooting my own short films in the big NYC. I'm thinking traditional and brooding B&W like the originals. And maybe, maybe some color vignettes with… man, I can't wait. For now, though, I got my ideas in my head. Sundance Film Festival aint ready for me. They aint ready.

Ma's left my mail on the bed. It's just us, but she won't open anything with my name on it – even when she knows what it's likely about. University needs my deposit and I'm due for a few court appearances to report my service hours working with the youth at the rec. They also want to know where I'm at with my restitution. Where I'm at is hoping my big mouth didn't share too much today. Nell isn't likely to share my… secret, but I shouldn't be so loose with information.

I'm looking for a clean record going into school and I don't need the university checking up on my past. The timing really was everything… when I applied, I wasn't a *convict*. I was just Tru Pitre. And now? Is it lying not to divulge a temporary setback? Judge said he'll expunge my sheet – erase it when my debt is paid. Ma is working a 24-hour clock and I'm putting in work with Ma Vee whenever I can.

More important, Jo is safe out there. She and Ma Nicolas are free of Erik. And someday, she'll hit me up and let me know everything that's happened since they left. Except… she doesn't know where *I* am.

Damn.

***

Nell is already in Ms. Yashar's room when I return for round two of our planning session.

"Sorry about yesterday," she says before I can even say hi. I notice she's returned to her usual curly hairstyle, so I assume the mood has changed.

"You cool?"

"Yes." She looks me straight in the eyes and I'm stunned. She's never looked directly at me. "So… you said no addiction."

"No. Too many addictions, too likely to be every group's topic."

I'm transfixed by her tapping pen. The beat is sporadic, but I'm thinking of lines to accompany it. She's silent. Thinking.

"Tru, Nell. You need to get on with it. All topics are due tomorrow. Tick tock." I forgot Teach was in the room. And I didn't think she was paying us any mind when she was. Did she hear us yesterday? I'm wracking my memory for what I said. Loose lips.

"Depression." I offer it up and Nell shakes her head immediately.

"Abuse," she replies. It stings.

"Abuse of?" I press her to expand.

"Well… spousal abuse? No, dating abuse. Teenage dating abuse. Is that too broad?"

"Too close to home." I mumble it, but she perks up. She's heard me clearly.

"I get it. Was it your mother? Sister?" Nell is speaking softly, leaning toward me.

"Friend. A really good friend, actually." I notice Ms. Yashar isn't browsing through whatever it is she's always looking at online. She's probably trying to listen, but this aint show and tell. "How about bullying?" I raise my voice a little, and when I look over at her desk, Teach is back to clicking on her keyboard and is also flipping pages in a textbook.

"What about it?"

I think I might be misinterpreting her tone, so I'm chill. "Ai'ight, Nell. Help us out here."

"I'm agreeing. Bullying is a good topic, but it's too broad. Let's simplify."

"Bet. You jot down a few subtopics and I'll do the same."

We're still both scribbling on paper when I hear Ms. Yashar's phone chime. She glances at a message and stands abruptly. "Okay, you two. I'm closing up the room." Ms. Yashar begins filling her bag with folders. She jangles her keys as if to hurry us along.

"Why don't we exchange numbers," Nell suggests, as Teach marches toward the door and stands impatiently at the light switch. Nell's holding her cell, ready to add me to her contacts.

"Naw, we got time in the morning. I'm'a make sure I'm here early." She nods, looking at me with a skepticism I'm used to. Right now she's wondering what my deal is — why I'm not dropping her the digits. I decide this still aint time for confession.

"Uh, okay." She says it reluctantly.

Ms. Yashar sucks her teeth and begins to tap her heel. I nod at Nell, grab my bag, and salute Teach at the door as I pass her. I leave my ideas on the desk, assuming Nell will snatch them up when she gets her stuff together to go home.

***

Dear sista
   I miss ya
         Your laugh, your smile, your glow.

Dear sista
   I miss ya
         Our talks, our time, our flow.

Dear sista
   I really miss ya
         Wish you could come back home.

Dear sista
   I really miss ya
         These streets are colder alone.

Jo's on my mind tonight. I wish I could get ahold of her — be assured she is ok.

It rained for six days straight after she left. Sometimes it was that misty rain that swirls and turns before it reaches its target. At other times, the rain came in diagonal sheets, obscuring visibility and drenching anyone unfortunate enough to traverse outside to reach his destination.

Yeah, it's sappy, but I found the weather cathartic, like Ma-nature knew I was feeling some kinda way and I couldn't shake it. I'm too grown to cry but holding it in is hard sometimes. No use frontin', I gotta let it flow. Rain's good for that.

I took a walk outside and let it pelt me, soaking my kicks and my fit as I moved along. I let my hoodie drop down so I could feel the cold bullets against my skin. I think I love her. My best friend from the playground, my sister from another mister, my A-1. You know - the girl that's perfect for you, but she's been your fam so long that she's not *your girl*, but your girl?

As I walked, I was alone on the street, save my thoughts that insisted I hear them. I didn't have any place to walk to, so I just headed down the pavement. If I walked with a purpose, no one questioned my steps. If I walked too slow, just sauntered along, cops would find my behavior suspect and I'd be confronted. I stayed away from LEOs as a general rule; patrol didn't need a reason to look longer my way and I wasn't gonna give them one. Jo couldn't hit me up. She and her mom's safety depended on it – a new life, no connects to this one. Erik ('round here they said it like *irk*, and that he did) was gonna be looking for Jo. Her mom's boyfriend wouldn't let "his harem" leave free and clear. You heard me, he called them *his harem*. Jo said he never touched her like that, but he definitely laid hands on her. And prayer don't leave bruises.

First time I saw Erik's mark on her, she was swinging at the playground.

"Come on, Tru. Push me!" She laughed as she swung, her two French-braids swaying toward heaven as she pumped herself higher. I came closer and went to slow her down by grabbing the ropes, but I caught her arms instead. She winced as I touched her, and when I pulled back my hand in surprise, I saw the purple and green hues peeking out from the cover up makeup she'd put on.

"Jo?"

She said nothing but averted her face from potential scrutiny. I walked around to look at her head on. "Jo, wha—" I saw her clearly, then. The concealer couldn't hide the swell, the evidence of a black eye threatening to mare her face. She looked at me, eyes glassy with unreleased sadness and said nothing.

Then she shrugged. "Push me, Tru."

I did. She didn't have to tell me it was Erik. I knew.

There was no confiding from Jo. She wouldn't speak at all except to say "Higher, higher!" each time my palms connected to the small of her back.

Anger surged in my gut. I gritted my teeth as I thought about it – speculated at the extent of Jo's abuse.

Erik had been her mom's steady for years. He moved them into his crib right after hooking up. It's probably why Jo and Ma' Nicolas put up with so much from him. Rent was high, landlords were shady and all about their ends, and available apartments were far and few between. Ma' Nicolas worked a 9-5 for minimum wage; it barely covered necessities and at month's end one bill was always on hold for "next time." Eviction notices at the Nicolas house came almost as routinely as the tiny paychecks.

Erik swept in like a … devil in disguise. And Ma' Nicolas felt her burdens relieved with his support. I wonder when he started abusing her.

And Jo? Damn, Jo. How much had he done to *you*?

I didn't push for her to confess Erik's sins, but I knew they were stacked.

"Tru?"

She'd been trying to get my attention for a minute - I could see it in her look. I'd all but stopped pushing her and as the swing slowed, she dug her sneaks into the soft dirt and let the last of the momentum drag them along.

"Yeah, Jo? 'Sup?"

"I …" her voice cracked and she cleared her throat before starting up. "Erik's hurting Mama. You know he drinks. He smokes. And when he comes in from his *'bih*-nezz'…" she mocked his speech then but looked cautiously around as though he might hear her and react.

Shivering, she bowed her head. The wind seemed to pick up suddenly, and I instinctively moved to rub Jo's arms, but stopped. I didn't dare touch the tender bruises and risk hurting her.

"It's getting cold. I'd better go home."

"Jo, wait. Talk to me."

"Later, Tru. Love ya."

I thought about pleading with her, about trying to get her to stay and tell me more but as she blew me a kiss and smiled, I just reached up my hand to catch the air born peck like always and said nothing.

She jumped up from the swing and hustled off in the direction of Erik's duplex. I sat on the swing for a long time after she disappeared from my sights, not really swinging, just thinking.

Back home, I tried call her, but my ring went straight to voicemail. I figured it was late, so I left her a text and pulled out my writing pad. With Tupac's *2Pacalypse Now* in my headphones, I penned a few lines. Writing helped me think and I needed a plan - something to help.

Erik's reign over his harem was gonna be cut short.

Reign of terror

Ends right now, right here

In no kingdom is this okay

Grave condition — leads to the grave

No longer can the rule rain down

***

I don't know what's wrong with me. I can't sleep and staring up at this ceiling isn't … productive. I'm gonna suffer for this bout of insomnia in the morning. I've spent some time jotting lines for a verse, but right now I'm craving some social connection. Times like these, I miss my phone – scrolling through photos and comments from associates and randoms (and the occasional friend) for hours to pass the time. Crazy that I'd miss something so inane, right?

I wonder what Jo is up to. About this time at night I could catch her at the playground. Streetlights are on, so the kids have booked home. But Jo? She'd linger outside well after most folks' curfew. She'd perch on the swing, dragging her feet slowly across the dirt to propel herself forward, then letting gravity pull her back. Sometimes, I'd sit in the next swing, keeping pace with her motion, and at other times, I'd push her. Damn, her laugh was infectious – sudden, honest, and powerful in the quieting streets. I could spend the whole night out there with her. It feels like a lifetime ago I got that money together in my pseudo Robin Hood front.

Hope she's cool, wherever she settled.

Erik was a nasty son-of-a… and Jo and Ma' Nicolas didn't need him holding them hostage. Aint no promise of a roof over your head worth his fists of fury and whatever other touching he felt free to indulge in. Jo wouldn't admit it, but I know he was trying to charm her - naw, to force her – to be his extra. If he didn't already succeed, it woulda only been a matter of time before his abuse hit a point of no return.

To be honest, his first hit *was that point* as far as I was concerned.

Jo tried hard to hide the evidence though I still don't know why she didn't tell me what was happening. Naw, that's not true – I know she didn't confide in me because she knew I wouldn't sit on the information. As soon as I saw her bruises, I was determined to get both her and her mama outta Erik's grimy hold.

I had a great plan for quick money - siphon chump change from electronic transactions. The client doesn't get charged; the company doesn't miss a few coins from their profit. I made the program in about a week of sleepless nights and set it up like a virus. And it worked like a charm — until I made one too many withdrawals in short time and an accountant noticed a discrepancy. By then, I'd gathered up what I called the "Nicolas and Dime relocation fund" and Ma' Nicolas and Jo stole away one evening while Erik was hanging on the block.

Jo' texted me when they settled that first night. "Got a spot to sleep. Movin' on in the A-M. ♥¡Ω" Her code for "I love you to the end."

Then my plan went left and I found myself held up. Ju-vee. Court. Newspapers reporting about a computer hacker stealing money in a get-rich-quick scheme gone awry. One of the reporters called me a "young genius," a description I rather liked. No one asked my story (lawyer wouldn't let me set 'em straight, no way) and only thing keeping me outta permanent infamy was that I'm a minor and they can't broadcast my 4-1-1.

Tonight is rough. Hate to admit it, but I'm feeling a little lonely. Isolated. Out of place. I need to vent about this school. These judgmental kids. This teacher, Ms. Yashar who won't let up. About how my ma is *killing* herself to repay my theft and free us both of this sentence. She won't let me work it off.

"School — that is your job. You graduate, go to university, and make movies," she says.

I see the strain in her face -the deepening wrinkles edging her eyes, the dark circles resting heavy on her cheeks. Putting her through this was not my intent. She's suffering because of me. My guilt is dragging behind me daily.

I almost talked to Nell about it. She asked about my "apprehension" with doing this PSA on abuse. She don't need to know about Jo's business with Erik. Or about why I'm here.

Nell's nice enough, but she's got her own baggage from what I peeped in that moleskin of hers. Besides, that is Jo's story to tell.

Maybe I should pop another tape into the VHS. I haven't watched any of ol' Chaplin or his contemporaries in a bit. Comedy gold and solid cinematography without the frills. I'm guessin' classics don't lure anyone to make 'em into DVDs, but these old tapes are fragile.

We don't have cable. Can't stream videos because, besides the cost, that requires internet connection and judge says that aint allowed. I can't even get on a computer to edit film, so I haven't shot any in a minute. Late night editing sessions used to be productive in the quiet – with no interruptions from loud neighbors passing through the hallways and less pedestrian street traffic.

Who am I kidding? In this neighborhood, there isn't much noise *ever*. It's too quiet. People seem like they're all part of a silent film. No arguing couples on the sidewalks. No kids at play in the streets. No hallway hoodlums shouting into cellys about hooking up or crooning lyrics or tapping beats against the walls as they strut through.

So here I am, watching the light flickers across the ceiling as the car headlights speed past the building. I probably should've taped up the cracked plastic curtain so the light couldn't leak in, but tonight it was creating intrigue for my eyes.

***

This melancholy got me trippin' and my pen is suffering. I mean, this took me like an hour and I'm jai like embarrassed that it still aint nothing worth sharing.

Black night. I aint alright.

Alone with my angry thoughts:

I see her pain

I can't ignore

Thinking about the marks

Blue and black on brown

No fight against his fists

She's no match for his fury

Hittin' a woman don't win glory

She hides her tears, covers his marks

Ashamed 'cause she thinks she caused his crazy

His daddy didn't teach him

You don't hit a lady

I see her pain

I can't ignore

Aint right the way he treats her

But rent's too high and jobs pay low

He buys her home; in exchange she takes his blows

Blue and black on brown

No fight against his fists

Black knight gonna make it alright.

She's crippled by fear but gotta escape

Getting away is the only risk worth a take

I have gotta shake off the blues. Baby girl is fine – Jo is resilient and
I just know she and Ma' Nicolas are probably settled in some fancy digs
in another state. They haveta be… or this aint worth it.

Nell

When she arrived to class in the morning, Tru was sitting casually on top of his desk, reading. It was early, still, and as she predicted, the class was otherwise empty.

"Morning." She tried to sound chipper, but that attribute was never hers to claim. She looked Tru over – the same white tee and jeans he always wore, well-worn shoes.

"'Sup?"

Ms. Yashar wasn't in the room. Odd, because she hardly seemed to trust Tru even though he'd never given her reason to determine he was dishonest. Certainly, he was no thief. A bit of a clown in class, yes, but not really the deviant student she seemed to have him pegged as.

"I was thinking about our topic," Nell said. "We agreed on bullying, but what if we did something about the family as the bully?"

"How? It's easy to point out school bullies and the results. But family? Family matters is private."

"Imagine having dreams - - plans that don't agree with what your parents want you to do."

"Ok, I feel you. Keep going."

She hesitated. To sell the topic, she'd have to be specific. "You know, you become your own person and it's the opposite of what your father or mother envisioned."

"Hmm? Naw, I don't follow. You mean career choices?"

"No." More hesitation.

"Nell, what are you tryin' to say?"

"Like… being authentic."

"How's that lead to bullying?"

Ms. Yashar's heels click-clacked in the hallway, warning them of her proximity to the classroom. She walked in briskly but halted as she saw her room was occupied. "Well, you two are early this morning. Have you made progress on the project?"

"Well, yes. We're meeting this afternoon to do research." Nell looked at Tru and shrugged. "At the public library. Is 4 o'clock okay, Tru?"

"Um, yeah."

She didn't mean to put him on the spot, but she needed time to plan her pitch for the project. She was going to have to tell him about Aidan.

"Tru, get off that desk's top." Ms. Yashar snapped as she resumed her brisk walk to her desk. Nell thought she heard her mumble "disrespectful" or "disgraceful" but she wasn't sure. "I'm looking forward to seeing what you two come up with," she continued in her usual volume tinged with skepticism. Except that if she felt that way, why had she suggested Nell pair up with him?

She didn't try to hide it – Tru could do nothing right in that woman's eyes. Nell was certain their teacher would never approve of him or his work no matter how good. Moving their meeting to the library – and away from Ms. Yashar's scrutiny – was probably the most merciful surprise she could have given him.

***

She stood in the full-length mirror, admiring her effort. The stark black leggings, black V-neck shirt that hit just at the curve of her hips, the fringed sleeveless jacket. She'd rescued it from a pile of Aidan's clothes that her mother had stripped from his meticulous closet. It was vintage suede with carefully laced collar-trim in a contrasting leather.

For a moment she lamented that she didn't have earrings. Then she held up her loose curls atop her head with her hand. The sloppy result looked effortless and was exactly what she wanted. She pinned it up with a clip. Making a duckface, she glossed her lips with a peppermint smelling balm.

She stood sashaying, letting the jacket's fringe sway and her curls bounce. She smiled, then. And laughed – imagining his voice calling out approval: "fab-u-lous dah-ling! My baby sis gets it from her Aidan."

Instead, she heard him – gruff and deep from the doorway. "Where do you think you 're going? What is with your hair?"

She startled. Crestfallen instantly, her shoulders drooped. Avoiding her father's condescending scowl, she straightened her posture and breathed deeply. *If I say nothing, he will leave. If I speak, he will continue his critique.*

Silence. Nell waited for what seemed like forever, holding her stiff posture in defiance. She would not give him the satisfaction of a verbal exchange. It was as though he craved confrontation and with Aidan gone, she had become the target of attack.

It had been months since she'd cared about how she looked. And while she was never one to dress to impress, Aidan had encouraged her to dress as *empress*. "Wear your power in your wardrobe. Challenge them to test your fierce. You are awe-some, girl."

"To hell with him and his unsolicited commentary," she whispered, wiping a tear off her cheek. "Get it Nell. Be fab-u-lous on the outside to match the inside. I hear you, Aidan. I got it."

Checking her watch, she set off to meet Tru at the library. She insisted on meeting off campus – away from the school's library with its aging titles and scrutinizing staff. Sure, it was some distance to get to the public library at the edge of town, but the staff minded its own business unless *asked* for assistance.

Nell arrived first, settling on the exterior steps with her satchel propped against her leg. Pulling out her moleskin, she began sketching the passersby.

She wasn't sure if Tru would be on time, but she'd never seen him late to class, so she knew instinctively he wouldn't make her wait long. *Unless agreeing to partner with me was some joke?* She shook her head, physically erasing the thought. *He needs this grade.*

Just then, the clattering bell of a pushcart sounded. She turned her attention to a little girl below her on the steps who was pointing at the cart and pulling on his shirt. He didn't speak but moved to hold the child's hand and led her down the steps to choose a frozen treat.

Nell flipped a page in her book and began sketching the pair. Tru arrived as she started on the details of the frizzy-haired vendor.

He stopped a few steps below where she sat, huffing a bit from his rush from the bus stop. "'Sup, Nell?" he said it without looking at her and didn't wait for a response. He was already ascending the stairs.

She closed her book, saving her place with the attached braided string bookmark, and turned toward Tru. He'd stopped his climb.

He stood admiring the columns reaching upward to support the guardian statues standing in their robes. The arched entryways appeared 60 feet high and each was topped with an ornately carved head. He could see the brightly lit interior from the three large windows placed over wooden doors that were surrounded by white stone. Nell walked up behind him as he stood transfixed by the impressive architecture.

"There's much more inside, Tru. Have you never been here before?"

"The library? Yeah, all the time."

"*This* library, Tru. Have you been to this one? It's magnificent, isn't it?"

He framed the building with his hands, turning toward each direction while squinting one eye nearly closed. "Naw, never come out here."

"What are you doing?" she looked at him, his fingers still fixed to form a rectangle as though he were taking a mental snapshot of every crevasse. When he didn't answer, she hesitated to interrupt, deciding finally to continue up the last few steps without him. "I'll be inside," she said more to herself than anyone else "if you ever want to see the place."

Nell couldn't understand the fascination with the building, but she remembered Aidan's tendency to wander off in new places to admire – no, to *soak in* – the sight as though he needed to hold it for later recall. Aidan always saw the beauty in the most mundane scene and if he didn't have his camera to capture the image, he'd try to recreate it for her later in words. She wondered if Tru had someone he'd share his "visual candy" with later.

Smiling, Nell found herself liking Tru's similarity to her brother. She hadn't felt comfortable around anyone in a very long time.

"Yo! You left me." Tru, suddenly at her side, jokingly chastised. They walked into the building side by side. "I could shoot this place!"

A nervous librarian looked up with alarm, but Tru was oblivious to the effect of his declaration.

Nell snickered at the reaction, then slowing to reassure the worried woman as she passed her, said, "With his *video camera*, ma'am. You know, film student."

The color that had drained from the librarian's face returned. "Of course." She nodded, but her strained smile betrayed her concern.

Shrugging, Nell sped her pace toward Tru, who was wandering through the rows some distance away. He looked strange, fingers tracing the book spines as he slowly browsed the collection. Occasionally, he'd stop, pull out a book and mouth the words of the title before replacing it. *What could possibly have intrigued him?* Nell wondered. She knew he always had some book with him in class, but he hardly struck her as an avid reader.

"Hey Tru? There are computers and workspaces that way," she said finally, pointing. "we should probably claim a space."

"Huh? Oh, yeah." Reluctantly, he turned toward her, still holding the last book he'd pulled. She noticed it was a volume of poetry, its cover a vibrant splash of colors with a bold print title emblazoned across it.

Nell settled at a computer workstation and opened the browser to a search engine. She motioned the chair next to her, "All yours." He started forward, then hesitated and retreated a few feet from her.

"Naw. I'm'a work over here." He picked a large striped chair near an empty table and set his bag on it. "This is good. I'll see if I can find a book or two on the shelves. Better yet... a few magazines."

Did I do something wrong? Nell shrugged off the thought and set to finding the required statistics for the project.

"This is a great spot, Nell." He had slumped into one of the large love seat style loungers. He was flipping through a periodical and jotting down notes on a pad next to him on the chair arm. She noticed his handwriting was meticulously neat.   "No real time constraints. No heel tapping clock watcher scrutinizing my movements."

"She is kind of harsh, isn't she?"

"Kind of? She's had me on criminal surveillance from jump. Can't take a joke. Obsessed with compu-class participation. What happened to person-to-person communication?"

"What's wrong with the online assignments? It beats the group ... discussions." *Shoot, now he's going to think I don't want to work with him. Awkward proclamations, as always, Nell.*

"Pen and paper encourage better product, ya'know? I'd think with all that journaling you do, you'd feel the same way."

She placed a hand protectively on her satchel with her moleskin tucked inside. He wasn't looking at her. "*Humph.* Maybe," she conceded.

No phone… no computers… There's got to be more to it than preference, right? She didn't dare ask, yet, but her curiosity about the truth of Tru was definitely perked.

She would save her inquiries for another time.

Tru

Back in class, Ms. Yashar is doing her usual peppy promos of the day's agenda: "For today's discussion, you'll be in new learning groups. You know how I like to switch it up. Then, there'll be time to work on the public service projects with your partners. And for the last twenty or so minutes, you'll work on drafting a response to the assigned reading." She points to each task on the white board, then adds, "Polish the response and post it tonight in the digital classroom, as always," and taps her fingernail against the assignment she's written on the board.

Teach knows I'm not going to do the online work but I can't help myself – I remind her. "I'll be sure to have it for you in the A-M." I stand and bow before sitting again. She raises an eyebrow at me silently, not entertaining a retort. I was looking forward to our daily comedy skit. What gives?

Nell hasn't looked up from her moleskin since she plopped into the chair. She's dressed like she was at the library – all in black – but something about her looks… I dunno… different. I have no doubt she's listening intently to the class interactions from her seat at the back of the room.

Yesterday, we'd wrapped up our separate work sooner than I think she was expecting. When I looked at my watch, it was already well past time for me to book it to the subway. I had to get to the community center for a few hours with Mama Vee. I was gonna be late for my scheduled service, so I didn't bother explaining to Nell. I just grabbed my bag and said "Catch you later, Nell. I got plans."

She'd looked surprised and stammered, "Uh… okay?" as I hustled away from our workspace and out of the library. I probably should've told her what was up, 'cause I think she read my actions wrong.

Now today, she is periodically shooting me looks. I can't read her expression.

Ms. Yashar's set a timer to sound the end of each segment of class and by the time we get to our allocated partner time, class is almost over. I pull a chair up to Nell's desk when she doesn't make any effort to move from her seat.

"Hi Nell, you okay?"

"Yeah, fine." She doesn't look at me. "You left in a hurry yesterday."

"About that. I should explain."

"No need. Sorry I kept you out."

Wow. She is salty. I don't know why, but I think she was hurt by my abrupt departure. No new connects, no attachments – that was the idea for this partnership. But if we're gonna get this project done, she can't spend the time in a funky mood. The tension! I gotta give her something. What could I share? There were too many people nearby to go into details about my schedule, but I needed to fix whatever snub she thought I'd made.

"I should apologize."

"For?"

"I had an appointment to make. I work in the city a few days a week and was on schedule yesterday."

"Why didn't you say you were limited on time?"

The Pom Pom Posse is looking in our direction, and Claire is leaning forward with obvious amusement, listening. "Aww, Nell, did your date get cut short?" They laugh.

Nell scowls.

What is it about people interrupting with assumptions? They know there's nothing going on with me and Nell except this project. And Zeke made it clear the whole class knows her story, so…

"Nell, I'm sorry." It probably wasn't the best response. It doesn't end the audience participation of the 3-P pains.

"Nell's sorry too. Trust me." Claire, again.

Nell's fist pounds the desk and she stands. "You… you…" She storms out of the room with Teach calling after her.

"Nell?" she searches the faces of her students. Claire, who tries in vain to cover her smile, looks quite smug. "What did you say to her?"

"You know Nell," Claire shrugs. "She has a flair for drama. I didn't say anything."

"Like hell," I say it quiet, but in the silence of the spectacle, Teach hears me clearly.

"Tru, out." She points to the door. "I should've known it was *you*."

I didn't need her invitation, I was already on my way out to find Nell. She was seated on the steps at the end of the hall, leaning back so that her elbows and back supported her weight. I scanned her face for emotion, but there was no expression.

"So, what kind of work do you do?" she asks as I settled next to her.

"It's my community service requirement. Been working for Mama Vee at the rec in my hometown since my sentence."

"Sentence? I don't understand. Does it have something to do with the abuse you mentioned? Your friend, right?"

"Jo. Her name is Jo."

"What happened?"

She looks at me to continue but I have serious reservations about talking. Erik was Jo's business, really, and I'm no snitch. But there is no harm in Nell knowing about my crime, so I decide to give her the story of robbing the 'hood to pay the piper and lead Jo and Ma' Nicolas to safety in a new apartment. I finish up the short version of my lawlessness as the bell rang and the halls fill with urgent students escaping the classes.

"Meet at the library again?" Nell calls after me as I set off to my next class. There is no judgement in her expression.

"Yeah, same time."

I gotta admit it, Nell's cool. She'd have been the kinda girl I'd hang with if I were putting down roots here but this is a temporary spot. The university room deposit has been sent and graduation is around the corner. New York here comes Tru.

Nell

This time, she didn't wait for Tru outside the library. Instead, she returned to the same spot they had settled in before. She made sure there were two computers free, but it was pretty clear Tru wasn't going to use one. *It's like he's a conspiracy theorist afraid someone is tracking his online activities,* she mused. Except his fears had foundation.

He'd already confided in her about his court sentence – no internet accessible devices, no online footprints. It was a pretty odd restriction, but she understood Tru had big life plans and needed his record expunged if he was going to fulfill them.

It was two minutes past five when Tru tapped her on the shoulder. "'Sup, girl?"

He was in good spirits. *Confession is good for the soul. I should try it.* Nell snickered and Tru raised an eyebrow.

"Somethin' funny?"

"No, not really. I was just thinking that you're in a particularly great mood and I'm probably vibing like an emo reject, as always."

"Well, you got no reason to fake the fun, considering what you've been through. Last thing class needs is another phony. Be true to you – you deserve it."

It hadn't dawned on her that someone in the class might've clued him in on her history. "Yeah… I suppose I do."

"So, you gonna tell me about it, or do I have to keep sneaking looks at that moleskin?" He said it so nonchalant, as though it weren't a significant invasion of her privacy.

"What?" She studied his face; he started to smile, looking straight back at her.

"Your book. You're always sketching or writing in it… what is it, like a diary or something?"

"Or something, yeah." *This is your opening, Nell. What's the harm?* She pulled the book from her satchel and gingerly flipped a few pages. "It keeps me sane."

Tru reached out a hand. "May I?"

No one had ever looked at her sketchbooks. She kept them semi hidden beneath blankets in a trunk in her closet. Handing him the moleskin felt somehow freeing. "It's mostly thoughts about Aidan. He's – well, he was – my brother."

"Yeah, I heard he'd passed… was it this last fall?"

"Yes. But he was dead to my parents before that."

"Family bullies?"

"Dad wanted an athlete. He wanted his son to bring home a pretty girl for Thanksgiving dinner. He wanted grunt matches and muscle flexing – a man's man with no dispute."

"I feel ya. Aidan wasn't man enough for your folks? Is that the thing?"

"Aidan was obsessed with fashion – if he couldn't buy what was in style, he'd sew it up himself. Every day he had to be über fashionable and that usually didn't include sports jerseys, sneakers, or jeans. He dressed for the runway of life and strutted better than the catwalkers. I envied his closet. And Chay is a guy I'd gladly call brother-in-law. Smart. Handsome. Polite. He treated Aidan like royalty and the two of them were a model couple."

"So…?"

"So Chay wasn't invited to cross the threshold of our home and Aidan was given an ultimatum. My mother was silent as he left. She didn't even hug or kiss him goodbye. And my father declared we were better off without him."

Tru was flipping slowly through the sketches, nodding. He stopped at a page, held it up for Nell to see the sketch he'd scoped in class. "Is this Aidan?"

"Yes." She smiled with pride at her brother's image.

"Looks like the life of the party. Cool peeps."

"He was awesome. I miss him so much." *Don't cry, Nell, keep it together.*

"I'm sorry."

"Me, too…" she whispered it, not intending for Tru to hear.

He exhaled loudly. "So, if you don't think it's gonna ruffle your folk's feathers, I'm cool wit' focusing on bullies. I got an idea."

Tru

Mama didn't stop him from running

His race to be himself

He ran toward love —

Knew love with a new love

Running from rejection

Misdirection.

Love's imperfection.

False start at home, daddy firing the pistol.

Blood aint always thicker, sometimes it can't feed the soul.

Waters sometimes richer, so he ran.

Pounding pavement with each sole.

Nell

Tru's idea was to build their video around family disfunction. "I think it's always the father who's vilified in flicks. What if the mom in our piece rejects her child? Wouldn't it be *power* if she was the driving force to our character's exodus?"

"I dunno. Sounds like you have been reading my journal. Let me think about it a little more?"

"Bet. Are you worried about your mom being put off by this?"

Nell flinched as though he'd touched her. Did she care that much about her mother's feelings? She hadn't spoken to her mother – or thought of her by that title for some time.

Aemelia, whose friends called her Lia, is all about creating appearances and managing perception. Her hair is perfect and modern. Her clothes, designer. And her children? Well, they needed to be ideal students and social stars. Except Aemelia had Aidan and Nell, neither of whom met her very high ideals. When grams named her, she had it right. What kind of mother shuns her son? One whose name meant rival, of course. Like Mr. Necahual, she objected to – no, she was fiercely appalled by Aidan's proclivities. She expected her son to bare the gruff masculinity as his father. She dreamed of an athlete, but Aidan's bowling, despite earning him a scholarship, was hardly the sportsmanship she admired. She didn't think it brag-worthy as it wasn't a physically aggressive sport.

Aidan refused to go hunting with his father. Instead, he took down the taxidermized duck plaques that hung in the family room and replaced them with his own photographs of wild birds. He collected the suits and clothes gifted to him for birthdays and holidays, gathered the soccer cleats and other sports equipment and donated them to charity. But he tried to honor his parents' wishes without compromising himself. Principal's Honors in high school, president of several school honor societies. Then, Valedictorian. Dean's List in college. He was perfect.

Except, when he was a sophomore in high school, he fell in love with Timothy. Nell remembered his pronouncement of affection. He stood in the center of his room facing his mirror and practiced. "Timmy, I… think I want to be more than friends. No, that sounds cliché. Tim, you know we're best friends, and I…"

She sat quietly outside the door, her back leaning against the hallway wall as she listened to his pacing, and she wondered how Timothy could have this effect on her usually confident brother and make him so unsure. The next day, Aidan met with his best friend. He gave him his heart. And ol' Tim responded with a black eye.

That night at home, both Aemelia and her husband listened to a stoic Aidan explain how he'd clumsily slipped and hit his face into a table's edge in the cafeteria and how the entire lunchroom burst into laughter at his expense. There were no words of consolation. Aemelia looked at her son aghast, her hand pressed to her chest as though she had been the one embarrassed at school. And Aidan retreated to his room without dinner. When Nell went to tell him goodnight, as she always did before bed, she saw his eyes puffy, though tears had stopped some time before.

"Did you talk to Timmy?" she asked him quietly, hopefully.

"How did you…?"

"I'm sorry. I was listening. I…"

"He won't be coming by to hang out anymore, Nell. I don't think any of my 'friends' will." He air quoted as he scrunched up his face. Aidan shook his head, flashed a smile, and stretched out his arms, beckoning Nell forward for a hug. "Love you, little sis. It's okay. *I am okay.*"

She was in elementary school then and had no idea what was going on with Aidan. He said he was fine, so she trusted he was, though she worried about the green and blue hue of his swollen face.

Nell didn't have to search her memory for the moment Aemilia failed Aidan – failed both her children, actually. She failed frequently with her unrealistic expectations and demand. She scrutinized and chastised, nitpicked and insulted.

And when Aidan, years later on a break between college terms, confided about his love life (after he could no longer politely decline yet another society matchmaking attempt), she revealed that unconditional love only applied to status.

How could she convey this to Tru? How could she confide in this *stranger?*

Tru was looking at her now, head cocked slightly to one side and eyebrows raised in inquiry.

Inside the pocket of her moleskin's cover, she kept a note she had fished out of the rubbish can in the bathroom she shared with Aidan just after his eye was blackened. Like her, he kept his thoughts contained in a journal but unlike her, he often removed pages – a sort of cathartic act to release the feelings and let them go. This particular crumpled page carried with it the deep creases created when Aidan crushed and molded it into a tiny ball before discarding it. It should've been safe in the trash. Afterall, who checks the discards of the restroom? Nell. Desperate to know what secrets her brother harbored – why his muffled sobs could be heard well into the night, why his confident and oft-exaggerated personality was dwindling, why their parents were increasingly critical of his whereabouts and activities - she resorted to investigating Aidan by any means she could muster. Snooping became her J-O-B (justified obtrusion bout).

Andreas and Lia showed no signs of change – they were both their usual showings of perfection with beautifully landscaped home, immaculate grooming of person and property, and appearances at all the best social gatherings. It sickened Nell. Aidan rarely joined them on 'family' events now; she didn't know if it was by choice or lack of invitation. He'd said once, "It's a good thing our parents have standards. My social card would be so full if they didn't." And he laughed at his luck for no longer having to endure the neighborhood or company events. But dinners out and family exclusive trips? Surely Aidan should be with them.

Then Nell found the discarded page. She couldn't read it then, but she kept it. When she learned cursive, his page was the first she read.

Now, she smoothed out the note to read it again, this time aloud to Tru:

> "I've had it. Another night, another slight. He's refusing to acknowledge me now. It seems the counselor – who assumed she was doing right by me by calling home – told about today's ordeal in the café. Why can't people leave it all be? She told him to check on me – his son – because a bully had bested me. A bully. Would it mean anything to him if he knew it was my friend? That I coulda gone head to head with the kid if he was anyone but Timmy?
>
> Who am I kidding? It wouldn't have mattered at all. I lost a fight. I caused a fight – did she tell you that, too?

I finally built up the courage to say something about my feelings. About the heart flutters when we accidently brushed shoulders. About the way I lose myself in thoughts of his physique, his eyes with flecks of sawdust scattered over walnut. About how every conversation about who we were 'feeling' reminded me of why I was only interested in him. No. She wouldn't have known that my affection grew from our familiarity – pitching dreams and baseballs. Running laps and racing to the future. Kicking goals and kicking it at the movies. Playing video games and playing 'shy brother' - me as the front man talking to some girl about how Tim thought she was cute but was too shy to approach her. Or, zoning over TV and contemplating the depleted ozone layer.

And now that I've told him how I feel, he's lost to me. I'm without a best friend.

I am alone."

"I don't expect my parents to care about our project. They… Aemelia and Andreas would not understand the topic and surely won't get that this is about us."

"It's like that Nell? I'm hella close to my moms. Can't imagine not talking to her on the daily. She's my heart. She's… if not for her, I'd still be locked up."

"Locked up? Uh. You mean in jail?"

"Ju-vee. Juvenile detention, actually. But, yeah." He looked at her and saw the shock on Nell's face. "Aww. It's not like I killed someone. Honest, Nell. You don't need my whole saga, but it's all good. My record is going to be *poof,*" he raised his hands with fingers pressed together, popped them apart. "Gone."

"Do they – Ms. Yashar and the school – know about your sentence? About ju-vee?" she was whispering.

"Don't think so. And I'd like to keep it that way." He shook his head. "I'm off to New York for film school next year and the fewer who know my… trouble… the better." Tru studied Nell's face, wondering if he'd said too much.

"Oh." Nell nodded and a small smile teased her lips. "I think you know I am not one to gossip."

"Bet."

Tru

Loose ends. The problem with opening up to people is that you make loose ends. But I got a heart and I can't ignore people's pain.

Let me explain. Before I could leave school today to meet up with Nell at the library, I walked back into Ms. Yashar's classroom. She'd kicked me out so abruptly that I didn't have a chance to pack up, and I had left my verses. Well — not *mine*. I don't do the notebook thing. I left my 'Pac at my desk. I'm kinda particular about my book. It was a gift from Jo for my birthday way back — but it seems like yesterday when she showed up at one of my shoots. She knew I'd be concentrating on my frames, trying to make my vision a reality in film. So she waited on the side of the b-ball court for me to cut. I was working on a short flick about a guy in love with a girl way outta his league. In my skit, the girl was a player for an opposing ball club, which I thought added to the irony even though most peeps I'd cast for the roles wouldn't understand the wordplay.

Anyway, Jo stood casually on the sidelines like an extra on my set, with her hands behind her back watching with amusement, then with shock as the leads collide when the girl baller forces a collision.

Ordinarily, I'd have shooed her out of my frame, but her reaction was perfect for the scene.

" And… cut!"

Jo smiled as she strode up to me, one hand still suspiciously hidden at her rear. "This looks like a great movie, Tru. Will it be ready for competition?"

"Hope so. A little editing. A few more scenes. Not a lot left 'til done." Jo knew this submission was going to set me up for a ride through film school. I needed it to be genius.

"Alright now." Her smile broadened and she proclaimed, "happy birthday, bro!" as she swung her arm forward and presented me with a paper bag wrapped present tied with a bow.

I couldn't squelch my laugh. "Is this dental floss?"

"That's what I had, Tru," she shrugged and a little pout formed on her face. "Think of it as multipurpose packaging."

"You – girl. You somethin' else."

"Something good, right?"

"You know it, Jo."

"Go 'head and open it."

I slid off the floss and winked at her as I rolled it into a ball. "You want this back?"

"Jerk." She giggled as she pushed me playfully on my shoulder. Inside the paper was *The Rose That Grew From Concrete*. "Open it. Go on."

She'd earmarked a page, a poem called "Sometimes I Cry." And in purple pen, she'd written, *I don't have to cry alone 'cause I have you.* A few pages further she'd folded the edge of "If There Be Pain…" She added, *Always, Jo.*

"Damn. That's deep. This… this is… wow. Thank you."

***

So I had to get my book from the classroom. It was of critical importance.

Teach was sitting at her desk when I arrived. I nodded a hello in her direction and she pursed her lips in a smirk and reciprocated the nod before decidedly ignoring my invasion. I'd never seen her in glasses, but she was wearing them now and they made her look formal, somehow more serious than usual. Beneath the frames, her eyes were red-rimmed and glassy. A collection of crumpled tissues decorated the desk corner and she held one tightly in a fisted hand. She sniffled.

"Ms. Yashar, are you okay?"

I think she pretended not to hear me. I persisted. "Ms. Yashar, can I help you with anything?"

Her voice was hoarse when, finally, she responded. "There's nothing to be done, Tru."

"Ma'am? I know it's not my business and I'm probably the last student you want to talk to, but I... I can see something is wrong. Maybe I can help."

She gasped. I might've been too straight. "You're right, it is not *your* business." She dabbed her tissue at her nose and her body kinda rattled like she'd been ugly crying for some time.

"I'm sorry, Ma'am. I'll be outta your way soonest."

"What, no jokes? No Keystone Cop routine?"

"Doesn't seem appropriate, Ms. Yashar. But I would like to know who stole your joy."

"Joy? Ha!" she shook her head. "More like stole my life." She wasn't talking to me, she was looking at a letter and some photos.

"Pardon?"

"Nothing, Tru. I'm fine." But she said the last part uncertain, her voice trailing off into a sob.

I'm a sucker for a damsel in distress, even if it is 'ya sure ya wanna mess with Yashar.'

"Can I call someone in here for you?"

"No, Tru. There is no one."

"Ma'am, I feel kinda odd leaving you here alone like this."

After dabbing her eyes with that crumpled tissue, she held the bridge of her nose. "This headache. Ugh. Just what I need."

For a second I thought *I* was the headache she was referring to. She was wincing, though, so I clearly wasn't the cause.

"Ms. Yashar?"

"Yes, Tru."

"Are you sure there's nothing I can do for you?"

Her body went rigid. "Your PSA outline is due tonight at midnight. And you owe me a response to the online discussion board." Just like a switch, her sadness was gone. Replaced with the no-nonsense teacher.

"Nell and I are nearly finished with that project work."

"Good. What about your *individual* assignments?"

"I'll write them for you and you'll have them tomorrow."

"Posted?"

"Well, I can't do that, but you'll get them complete."

"Tru?" she was getting frustrated – her mood shifting further as she prepared to attack.

"I can't really explain, Ms. Yashar. I'll get you the work, but the online discussion board is not an option."

"Who are you to ---"

"Ma'am, with all due respect, I've always done the work. What does the delivery mode really matter?"

"Why should I make exception to expectations for *you*, Mr. Pitre?" Uh oh. Last name meant she was pissed. Or maybe she liked using it because she knew it meant clown – a sort of insult without obvious intent. She wouldn't be the first to throw my name at me once they looked up its translation.

I spoke in measured tones, trying to calm her before she could amp up the attitude. "I'm not asking for exception. I just hope you'll grade my work, same's you do everyone else's." She looked fully recovered from her bout with the blues and I was primed to bounce. This confirmed it for me: she'd be a dangerous confidant even if it would benefit me. "Well, I just came for my book, so I'm out now. Bye."

"That's not accepta—" I walked out as she started talking and didn't slow to catch the conclusion.

Loose ends. I suppose I coulda gotten her sympathy if I gave her my history lesson, but naw. Giving her the 4-1-1 would mean one of two things: either she cuts me some slack and lets me do my work without the online submissions or she digs into my case and puts my college plans in jeopardy. I can't risk the latter.

What was that she said though, about someone stealing her life? I'm intrigued. Teach got something going on in her personal life that I'm itchin' to discover.

No.

I'm'a keep my distance.

As it stands, my life is all about perfect timing. I'd applied early action to the university before I started my Nicolas crusade. I got the acceptance in the mail a few days after the judge's gavel pounded his desk and set my sentence firm. I didn't disclose my conviction – it wasn't until after I mailed my application that I got it, so I was never lying. The way I see it, they would have no reason to rescind my approval if my record was expunged by graduation. But if I tell this woman who obviously don't like my existence in her world what's up? She could stop my clock and ruin me with one phone call to admissions. That's power she can't be given.

Nell

Tru insisted their public service announcement be authentic, which meant they'd be filming.

Nell was skeptical. "Isn't that a bit involved for a class project?"

"We'll have to do it in one take, 'cause I can't exactly edit it except on a machine with no 'net, but I think it can be done if we script it right."

Then he'd rattled off some good ideas for their PSA and radiated confidence, so she agreed. *He knows the term grade is based on this*, she reasoned. Besides, if the whole class decided to take the easier route and create a poster campaign or something, Nell and Tru's work would easily stand out for the better.

She couldn't believe how accepting he was of Aidan's story – how he'd totally invested in setting her family straight with this assignment. "Love is love," he'd said about Chay and Aidan. "I don't know how any Dad could deny his child that. Naw, scratch that – I do. My pops aint stick around long enough to know me and decide to reject me, he did that *ish* in utero."

He was turning out to be an alright guy – someone she wouldn't mind talking to even if this project didn't exist. She'd figured out his affinity for filmography just from the way he had framed his view walking up the library steps. He really was like Aidan (who had liked still photography) although she couldn't picture Tru trading his jeans and tee for something in Aidan's closet.

"So, you don't care if we make this more of a Pride PSA?" She wanted to be absolutely certain he was prepared for all possible backlash. "I mean, you heard how Claire and crew talk. You don't want to be their target of assumption."

"Ha! First, they'd have to pry the target away from Teach – her scope's been trained on me from day one. But seriously, if you think I'll be marked 'Gay by association,' you aint got nothing to worry about. I learned a long time ago you gotta be true to yourself – to express yourself how you see fit and with whom you choose. I'm not trying to start a crusade with this or nothin', but I think your parentals need a lesson about acceptance and maybe, so does this school."

"Are people okay with LGBTQA+ where you're from? This town isn't exactly opening doors to welcome diversity, I'm sure you've noticed." She'd seen the critical looks he'd gotten when he arrived looking a bit too ethnic urban for the country club class.

"Man. In the streets, you get in where you fit in. Lady Coco's been dressing in drag for the cabarets she hosts since I was little and she's so good at beating her face that the girls come to her for makeup lessons. And there's George who lived in the apartment above mine. He liked to dance instead of walking – had a natural pep in his step. Folk used to tell Ma to keep me away from the fag – their words, never mine – or he'd rub off on me. I never could see what they were concerned about and Ma thought he was a great emergency contact when she worked late and left me home alone. As I got older, I realized the only thing different about George from other men is that he had a boyfriend. There are so many other colorful folk in the city – straight, gay and everything in between, each one trying to find themselves."

"You observe people a lot, huh?"

Tru smiled. "Don't you? True colors show when people stop pretending 'cause they think you aren't looking and listening."

Nell studied Tru. He'd relaxed into the chair, his arms laying on the rests. He wasn't like the guys in school at all. He seemed wiser – like he'd lived life, not been sheltered from troubles and heartache and failures. He'd been honest with her about the court sentences and his time in juvenile detention. *He almost gave up his future for Jo. Now he has no idea if she's safe where she's gone.*

"Earth to Nell. You okay?" He was snapping his fingers in a circular motion.

She hadn't realized she was zoning out. "Yeah, fine. I was just thinking about something."

He clapped. "Okay… so, we should probably get this outline together."

Nell opened up a word processing document and quickly typed in a page header. She titled their PSA "Truth: Without Consequence."

Tru continued, "Here's what I was thinking we'd do…"

They worked until the librarian announced through the speakers: "Ten minutes to closing. Please bring your selections to the checkout counter. We'll reopen tomorrow at 10 a.m."

At home that evening, she closed and locked her bedroom door. She searched for variations of "cyber genius" hoping to read up a little more on Tru's past. She didn't have reason to – he'd told her freely how he ended up here, but she couldn't help wanting to know more. *Maybe if I get the other side of the story, I can talk to Ms. Yashar and she'll be more understanding.*

If she could just explain that Tru wasn't being purposely defiant with his refusal to participate in the online classroom, Nell couldn't imagine their teacher would be so nasty toward him. *He's not disrespectful. He's following orders. How can she fault him for that?*

Nell continued searching well into the evening, extending her search parameters to include every major city in the state were a juvenile was charged or suspected with a crime. If the computer search turned up nothing, she was certain she could find more specifics of Tru's transfer from the office files – she just had to be a little resourceful to access them.

Tru

I was taking inventory of where I'm at today:

1. One month left at school.
2. A couple grand left on the restitution.
3. A hundred hours left of community service – I won't quit that when the time's up, though, 'cause Mama Vee needs me.
4. Four months until freshman orientation in the N-Y-C.

I cannot wait.

I had a talk with Ma last night at dinner. It's rare she's home at mealtime, but when she is, she throws down in the kitchen. It's nothing extravagant – we can't afford fancy – but e'rything is made one-hundred with love.

"Tell me about school, Tru. How's the 'burb education treating you?"

"Aint nothing like home, Ma."

"Isn't anything." She refused to allow him language shortcuts – *any* shortcuts, really. Proper language, proper behavior were the standards for the gentleman she was raising.

"Sorry, Ma. You know, I miss the old 'hood. Teachers who cared. Time at the rec without the hour-plus trip to get there. Shooting flicks of the city folk. Authentic people."

"Baby, this place is supposed to be good for you. For us. You've only a few months before you leave me for university. You have got to focus on your grades."

"Yeah."

"Yes."

"Yes, Ma. I hear you. My grades are fine. I'm doing my work. Not gonna chance losing my chance."

"I left the last letter from the lawyer for you, did you read it?"

"Yes ma'am. He was writing to tell me of the next review. Providing I'm paid off, the judge is set to clear the records."

She smiled at me, then covered a yawn with her hand. "That's good, baby. It's going to work out just right for you."

I'd had to tell Ma all about the dilemma after the cops came knocking. She needed to know I wasn't screwing up for a quick buck. I needed her to know that her son wasn't some no-good hustler with a future in lock up. I wasn't meant for a cell – I'm supposed to be in a dorm room.

As always was the case when I confided in her, Ma understood. She even said something about raising a stand-up young man. Yeah, she chastised my illicit methods but, she said, "your heart was in it."

***

Thinking back to my sentencing, I know I'm one of the lucky convicts. Calling myself that is still surreal. I am a convict. Judge gave me what some might call a 'pass.' I wasn't expecting it, but I'm grateful for it.

Compassion was not the vibe His Honor was giving during my case.

The stale smell in the courtroom was suffocating. That, and the tie that Mama Vee knotted so tight against my Adam's apple that it hurt to swallow was steadily choking me. To my left, the young brother assigned to represent me in my case tried to look confident, his posture erect like he was wearing a back brace, and his jaw set rigidly. I'd have thought he *was* certain of his work defending me, except he was sweating so profusely that he looked like someone had splashed water on his temples. I bet if he wasn't wearing a suit jacket, there'd be ever-expanding armpit stains decorating his button down shirt.

For a court appointed attorney, he was a'ight. I mean, he talked a good game laying out my case. Several in the small audience nodded whenever he gave them some part of my sob story – exaggerated for sympathy so much at some points that it only loosely resembled factual 4-1-1. What was that he said? Oh yeah, something like:

"Abandoned by his father, he lacked a strong male role model... He's product of a single, working parent... Was raised in a bad neighborhood infested –" he spat the word and twisted his face at the foulness of it "– that's right, infested with illicit activity: Drugs. Robberies. Violence... He is old enough to get a job, but who is hiring teenagers at an hourly rate worth the time?"

If there had been a jury, which there wasn't for my juvenile court case, he'd probably have sold them on my complete innocence. As it was, my biggest supporter seemed to be an older lady in the courtroom from the social services office, her skin sagging with years of life, eyes magnified by thick spectacles, hair a just-curled collective of white and silver strands. As he painted his portrait of *Fake* ('cause it wasn't really true), she raised her glasses with frail, shaking hands and dabbed at the corners of her eyes with a flowered kerchief. She must've known someone like this version of me he crafted.

The attorney for 'the company injured by my actions,' this one maybe 30 or 40 years old with a politician's air about him, sat with his hands clasped together in his lap as my lawyer spoke. His suit was pressed, his collared shirt buttoned all the way up. He was clearly unimpressed with the carefully tailored story. Occasionally, though, he leaned forward, clicking his pen open to note something on a steno pad for later recall.

The description of my life produced for the courtroom audience sounded like fiction in my ears. And some of it was damn offensive. I aint never been a charity case. I aint to be pitied. Ma did right by me. She made sure I was fitted, fed and functioning in school. She kept a roof over my head and respect in my words. And she blessed me with Mama Vee and my rec folk to extend the branches of our family tree.

"Despite the odds," he continued, "young Tru has excelled in his studies… his record is clean. This one indiscretion… one blemish on the white sheet of a law abiding citizen should not ruin his future."

Yeah, I'd have pegged my lawyer's conviction in me, his cause, except he made me out as some 'I didn't know no better way, suh' criminal. That is not a truth I will embrace even if, as he said, that is probably what led to the judge's verdict on a lesser series of charges than the ones the prosecutor was vying to stick me with.

Judge Kagan. My lawyer cowered before him whenever the man spoke – his voice deep and powerfully projected. His is an imposing presence – seemingly too large for his seat behind the abundant judge's bench, with his large square shoulders rigid under his robe. His oil slicked black hair was always perfectly coiffed on his head, his ears protruding below the closely faded temples, a bulbous nose positioned above a pencil-thin mustache and a permanent frown etched into his angular face.

Judge Kagan had a reputation for strict application of the law and imposition of long sentences to deter recidivism. My lawyer said he was fair – as fair as he could be within the confines of legal code. I would be found guilty. I would be sentenced. My future would be determined by this gruff, oversized man in the black robe and blue bow tie.

He lectured me for a long time before banging the gavel down – the weight of finality in a solid blast of sound that was amplified by the courthouse walls. I will never forget what he said. His words are forever recorded in my memory.

"Tru Pitre," he began.

My lawyer looked toward me as he stood at attention, silently willing me to rise next to him at the desk with his eyes and the slightest of head nods. Placing my hands on the desk, I willed my legs to stop wobbling. I don't know if it was my nerves or lack of use after the endless courtroom back and forth between the two lawyers.

"Young man, you have admitted to committing a serious crime – that of theft amounting to thousands of dollars. While I understand you believed your only recourse to save the lives of your friend and her mother from domestic abuse was to finance their relocation, stealing is never the solution. The law specifies that you must recompense the companies you have injured. Additionally, you must restore the community's faith in you through service. I hereby sentence you to pay restitution and serve 250 hours of community service. Until you repay your debt to society, you may not use any device that is connected to the internet – phone, computer, laptop, even game systems. You are to have no online presence. Tru, when this sentence has been satisfied, your record will be expunged. Do good, young man, do good always."

Mama Vee leaned forward, half-whispering but still loud enough to be heard clearly by most of us in the confined space. "Yes lawd!"

Behind me, Ma clasped her hands together and held them against her heart. She rocked slowly, her eyes closed, as she weighed the gravity of Judge Kagan's sentence.

***

"Any chance you've heard about Jo?"

"Tru, Ms. Nicolas and Jo ghosted. And that's probably what was best. No one talks about them or knows where they went off to. No need to worry, though, I'm sure they're doing well. Slimy Erik is still slinging poison on the corner. Has he approached you when you go to the recreation center for Mama Vee?"

"No'm. Haven't had reason to linger en route."

"Good, baby. You know I worry about you going up there at night." She stood over me, twirling my twists in her fingers and scratching my scalp. She kissed my forehead, then yawned again. "Just about time for my shift."

Then, she was up gathering up the dishes.

"I got 'em, Ma. You sit down until it's time to go. You look tired."

"Well, damn, Tru. That was cold. I know I'm not as young as I used to be, but I thought you agreed that your mama still got it."

"Ma!" She laughed, hands on her hips as she sashayed past me. "You know you're beautiful. Always the prettiest lady."

"Don't I *know* it."

I cleaned the kitchen before settling into the room to write up my discussion for English. Ms. Yashar is dealing with something deep, but I hope she isn't planning to take it out on me or mines because I walked in on her private classroom episode. I jai like want to know who stole her life – whatever that means. I also think staying out of her radar and her business is my best path to cap and gown glory.

And Nell? I think her real issue isn't that Aidan is dead. It's that her family don't know what unconditional love looks like. She can only do right by them if she does the right they demand. That's not living. She's one of those flowers – a wall flower in class and a wildflower at home. She aint fixin' to bloom in either place, though, if something doesn't give soon.

***

Concrete can't stop the wildflower

Seeking sunshine and sky

She breaks through the surface

To find freedom

Pushing through cracks in the foundation

To escape the blockade.

Wallflower waits

and watches

Climbs the bricks for a better view

Can't blend in

She's growing up

apart

The garden's too small

for her to thrive.

Nell

Class never seemed to change – at least the students didn't. Claire and crew were always comparing their latest labeled accessories, dishing about manicures and makeup, sharing schedules, or – and this was their favorite conversation – spreading gossip about some poor schmuck unworthy of traveling in their circle.

Until yesterday's intrusion, Nell had stayed out of relevance. She was not 'worth' mentioning, a non-entity taking up space in class. But now with her partnership on this project, they'd found something of intrigue.

"So… what's the deal with Tru and Nell," she overheard Carrie saying to Claire and Sue.

"No clue. There's no way she's turned *his* head."

"That melancholy mess couldn't turn anyone's head. Always bent over a book or nerd-salivating over some smart thing she can interrupt normal people with."

Nell, sketching caricatures of her tormentors, tried to seem oblivious to being the subject of their conversation. *Ignorant twits. Tru is so right, the 'Pom Pom Posse' isn't worth the energy of retort.* It dawned on her that were they to ever see her book, she'd be subjected to far worse attention than being topical. The girls were featured on several pages, their inner ugly showing outwardly.

Zeke interjected, "Ladies, ladies. Such… speculating. You know as well as us all that Tru was assigned to be her partner." He nodded toward Tru, who was too far away to hear. "So, where's the party at this weekend?"

And like that, the conversation shifted.

She smiled timidly at Zeke for his attempted save – even if it was at her expense, it had freed her from being the focus.

"Tru Pitre I did not get your discussion post." The routine was so predictable.

"I've got the work right here, Ms. Yashar, as I promised. Remember our conversation?"

Ms. Yashar winced and did not respond. *That's new.* Her heels clicked across the floor and she snatched Tru's extended papers.

Tru hadn't mentioned an encounter with their teacher, but clearly something transpired after Nell had left class. Maybe he told her about his situation, and she was finally being reasonable?

Her search for the "teen computer genius" had turned up several articles. It was, apparently, a common descriptor of hackers. Without knowing where Tru was from or who he'd hacked, there was little way to narrow down her search and none of the articles she found matched what Tru told her of his transgression.

She had considered starting a search for Jo, but she couldn't tell from the profiles she'd found which "Jo Nicolas" was Tru's. She'd have to figure out how to get a description from him. *Nosey Nellie flexing my investigative skills like Bly of the same name.*

But as she scanned the search results, there was a nagging feeling that maybe Tru's truth was best left unknown.

Tru

Tabula Rasa – the blank slate. It's harder to attain than I ever thought.

The past has a way of taking hold of you.

It steps on your shoelaces

and trips you up.

It pulls on the back of your coat

and forces you to shrug off the garment

to shake free.

It's persistent.

It leaves notes for you

to find and read.

It hides around corners

waiting until you draw near

so it can spook you.

The past aint ready to be erased.

In class we've started reading Octavia Butler's *Kindred*. The woman in the book goes back in time and is stuck rescuing her ancestor to ensure she can exist in the future. I can't figure out how she gets caught up trying to save this troublesome man from death over and over in different segments of his history. But once she saves him the first time, he keeps calling her to do it again like it's her debt to pay for wanting to exist. His past and her present are connected – one relies on the other.

And why does Teach got us reading this book about slavery? Nobody in this class seems to be strong on empathy or understanding. The book is kinda good, though. I gotta admit that I'm caught up in the story. If you take out the time traveling, *Kindred* mirrors life.

Nell and I are all set to start recording our script. I'm thinking about doing it in the old 'hood, but I still aint sure bringing her into my world is a good idea. The less she knows, the better it is to avoid connections. Even so, I'm watching the scenes pass by the window trying to plan out the best frames as the train speeds down the tracks.

It's a later train than I usually catch, so I miss Jingles' promenade through the car shaking his coin cup. When the train stops, I make my way briskly toward the rec. But as usually happens when you talk about someone, Erik is standing post on my route. Damn. Ma and I had conjured him up.

I keep my pace, destination in sight. I was due to help Mama Vee with another of her paint nights – the last one was a success and folk had been inquiring about the next one ever since. She expected me to set up and break down the workspace.

Erik looks up just as I cross the last street before the rec center. He was leaning against the brick of a building, smoke curling from his lips, one hand shoved in his pocket. At first, I didn't think he'd seen me. But then I saw him shift his weight off the building and advance.

My heart quickened, but my legs felt like lead. I didn't need this reunion tonight. I didn't need this reunion *ever.*

"What's good, Little Man?" he says as he gets within hearing distance.

I don't dare look his direction.

"Yo. I'm talkin' to you, youngin'. How's your girl Jo?"

He is walking incredibly fast for a smoker and at this point, could easy grab my jacket collar if he wanted to yoke me up. A car drives past slowly – too slowly – and the tinted windows drop down. "Yo E, let me holla' at you."

My heart quickens. *Is this the end?*

I'm looking at Erik and he's grittin' on me hard. He chucks his head once and says, "Lucky I got bi'nez to attend. I'll catch up wi' you later." He jogs to his customer and pokes his head into the window.

I wasn't waiting for their exchange to finish. Taking this as an exit cue, I hustle toward the center.

There's no tellin' what Erik's heard. Ma' Nicolas was his woman and if he suspected I'd been responsible for her... disappearance, it won't bode well for my health.

"Just in time, my Tru!" Mama Vee pulls me into her crushing hug. "I'm thinking tonight we'll have the kids paint a water scene – you know, the beach, some boats, those rainbow umbrellas, the Adirondack chairs?"

"Yeah, Mama, that sounds *nice.*" I try to sound excited, but I'm tensed up awful. Hell, I am scared. Erik could be waiting for me tonight and no good is going to come of it.

"Baby, you okay? You're trembling."

"Ran into a ghost of my past on the way here."

"Who?" She is holding my shoulders firm, her eyes peering into mine like she is reading my soul for lies. "Who?" She shakes me, trying to knock me back into focus. "*Humph*. No boy of mine gonna be fighting in the streets over what the hood has already buried. You betta tell Mama Vee somethin' chile."

"Come on, Mama. Let's get this class set up. How many you think are coming tonight?"

She stares into my eyes but releases her grip on me and shakes her head slowly as she backs away. "You boys and your pride. You can't take it to the grave."

The grave – *my* grave. If Erik held a grudge against me, he'd seek me out no matter how much time had passed. Could I chance his wrath?

I spend much of the class trying to help one of the kids get her paint onto her canvas instead of herself. She dropped her brush. Then she dipped her fingers into the paint on her paper plate palette and dabbed it everywhere. Hers was an abstract effort.

I catch myself watching the clock. Was it moving faster than usual? Taking my time washing the brushes in the sink, I contemplate my options. Do I tell Mama Vee my troubles – snitch – and hope she had a plan to ensure my tomorrow? Or, take a different route to the train? Could I dip out with someone with a ride? Ma is probably waiting up for me, so I have to get home.

Mama Vee hugs me again. "I love you, son."

Kissing her cheek, I make my decision. "Love you, too, Mama Vee. See you soon." I grab my pack and check the clock on the wall on more time. Trains were rarely delayed and mine is due in 20 minutes.

Outside, the streets are eerily quiet. I didn't see Erik in my quick scan, so I set off toward the station, keeping off the sidewalks and walking up near the trees. My ears are on high alert – listening for footsteps or cars. Nothing. I walk quickly, nearly jogging the last block to the train.

As soon as mine arrives, I slide past the few people exiting and walk through that first car to another. I sit down as the "doors closing" announcement piped through the speakers, breathing a sigh of relief.

Then, as I'm looking out the window as the train starts moving, I see him. Erik is standing at the end of the platform scanning the train.

I might have to lay low for a bit. Erik is obviously looking for me. I'm so close to finishing my hours and satisfying the courts, and now this.

Tabula rasa? Not when you owe a debt.

***

So Erik's got a beef with me. I could see it in his face. The tightness of his jaw, which twitched a bit at the corners. The glare from his eyes. Even the rigidness of his pose showed his aggression. His body was tensed like a coil pushed down against a hard surface – ready at any moment to spring. Yeah, he is pissed and I am the cause.

The hood talks. If I'd have stayed, I'd hear the convo. It used to be a source of entertainment to listen to the chatter. Especially in the barbershop. Haircuts take all day 'cause barbers like Unc and Cuzzo stop mid buzz, clippers hovering above someone's half-cut hair, to spread the news with anyone who'll listen. Theirs is a captive audience (aint no one leavin' with half a cut) so there are always ears piqued for the rumors. With me gone, my name is out their mouths and for most, I'm not even a memory.

Ma was right to uproot us - - even though it meant moving to a smaller place in a high-priced, bougie part of the burbs she can't hardly afford. But, she said, we couldn't afford *not* to relocate if I was gonna have a real chance at a future. And after this encounter with Erik, I'm certain my future is in jeopardy if I return. Maybe it's best to plant new roots.

I'm itching to get this film making shtick moving. I got dreams in the daytime to fulfill - can't sleep on my goals.

Where did I even stash my camera? Oh yeah, the box in the closet buried under my winter clothes. Box is looking a bit beat up – probably shoulda packed it better (or maybe not have thrown it into the back of a shared closet), but there it is, waiting for the season's change.

Damn. It's dusty back here. That's kinda odd, considering we aint been here long. I'm used to dirt and grime. What city doesn't have it? The soot from car exhaust, the mold-ridden carpets in decrepit apartments. Rusty fire escapes, discarded wrappers of every variety. And broken bottles shattered before some collector could make claim on the recycle deposit. I didn't think the dust in the burbs collected as quickly. I didn't think about *this* place at all, honestly. How could I?

***

When I get to the rec, Mama Vee is wringing her hands together with worry. She tries to smile at me when she sees me come in the door, but it is one of those smiles where the corners of her mouth twitch under the strain of the unnatural expression.

"Mama, what's up?"

She's standing behind the curved reception desk, watching the lobby with trained eyes. It's about time for the evening hoops matches and open gym, and in a little bit, I'm supposed to help her with the "Art Tags" program. The first two sessions were a big hit and Mama Vee turned it into a regularly featured class for would-be taggers to 'refine their skills,' as she says, before they pick up spray cans and mark up buildings.

"Tru baby, I… I have heard some things," she says slowly, coming around the desk to hug me.

"Should I be worried? Is it about Jo and Ma' Nicolas?" I feel my heart quicken and it is suddenly hard to breathe. "What is it?"

She shakes her head slowly, but she isn't talkin'. I can't read her expression.

"Mama, please!" Am I trembling? Why is she stallin'?

"You can't come up here no more." She grabs me by the arms and her fingers press into my biceps. "It's not safe."

"You're gonna have to tell me more than this – this is my home, Mama," I plead with her and she shakes her head with conviction.

"I'm not risking your future, Tru. I can't have another one of mine taken by the streets."

"The streets? I'm not in the streets." Then I realize what she's heard. Erik's been looking for me.

"You may not be in the streets, but the streets is into you. It aint safe here. We're gonna have to figure out another way for you to get your hours.

I'm jai like confused. What drug dealin' corner hustla wastes his time or his reputation searching up a dude over a woman? The only thing I know a guy like Erik to be pressed about is money. I didn't touch his stacks, and I didn't impede on his bi'nez. Jo and Ma' Nicolas's escape aint touch his rep. I wouldn't be surprised if he moved on as soon as they moved out.

Mama Vee is giving me a once over, scanning my face for my thoughts, but I don't think she's picking up anything in my expression other than confusion. "This isn't a negotiation, Tru."

"But Mama, I –"

"Let me stop you right there. Erik's got young runners trying to invade this rec. E'rytime I ID his latest recruit tryin' to implant himself – or herself – into my sanctuary, we run 'em out of here, but a new one shows up within days. The lure of quick money, the temptation of power is magnetic. Used to be that his crew camped on the corner selling poison, but they are coming inside now," she looks around the lobby, and I follow her scan.

I'm noting the folk lingering around, remembering suddenly that this is not a private space. Youngins' are looking for a come up and they get it sometimes by collecting dirt – information – on persons of interest, as the LEOs like to say.

There are 10 young men around the space and a few young ladies. Some seem to be lost in a cacophony of beats blasting from their headphones that are so loud, we could get our heads nodding to the residual sound. One girl has a speaker connected to her celly, and she and her crew are working on a cypher – spittin' freestyle over an instrumental track. I'm smiling as I listen; the girl's flow is solid and as she lays down lyrics, her hands conduct the rhythms and her body is grooving. Her curly 'fro joins the moving frenzy, as do her super-sized hoop earrings. A little man – no older than five – is tugging on his dad's jacket, and the man is trying his best to shoo him away.

But then I notice him – a guy who doesn't look like he's got reason to rest against the wall, his hands deep in pockets and his hood still up on his head even though he's inside the center. I avert my eyes just as quickly as they settle in his direction, but he caught my glance; I know, 'cause his eyes narrowed ever-so-slightly as though he was trying to place my face. Granted I'm not at the rec daily like I used to be, but he aint a regular here, far as I know.

I'm nodding at Mama Vee. I see him and so does she. She moves back behind the desk, her fingers trailing along a paper of office phone extensions for the rec staff. Finding the one she needs, she dials quickly. I can just make out a man answering, but she cradles the phone headset low behind the raised reception counter and does not move it to her ear. "Listen now," she says to no one in particular. The man on the other end of her call says something in reply that I can't decipher.

Waving her hand, she beckons me closer. "Tru, how 'bout you set up the 'studio' for our class? I'll be there in a few."

Her eyes widen and her brow raises when I don't immediately move, then she jerks her head toward the rooms where she teaches the classes.

I nod and walk briskly toward the room.

Mama Vee joins me shortly after I've finished setting up the palettes of paint and laying out wooden canvases on the tables. "I see you've read my notes on tonight's class?"

"Yes, ma'am."

"You like the idea, don't ya? We're going to install these wood pieces along the hall leading to the gym like a relief mural. Paint, reclaimed materials and creativity equals beauty." She is searching in the cabinets as she talks. Pulling out several containers of metal and plastic pieces, she continues, "been collecting the trash from around the center for weeks. Bottle caps, bolts, straws, screws and nails, springs – so much discarded. Let's make something beautiful out of what others have deemed unworthy."

It's more than a statement about art. Mama Vee likes to preach about the "value of her young people that society overlooks – or worse, casts aside." I love her for it. Pride in self and community is somethin' birthed at this rec daily.

"Bet. I like how you think, Mama." I'm wondering if I should ask about the dude in the lobby or about my name in the streets again. Inhaling deeply, my eyes closed, I weigh what I'm assuming will be her response in my head. If she says what I think she's going to – that Erik's got people lookin' for me at the rec so he can continue our 'conversation' – then she's gonna drop my community service gig and I'm gonna need to finish somewhere else. But this is my community. Where else can I serve?

"You mighty quiet, chile. Use that voice. Speak your truth."

"Huh. I feel like I been untrue since I left my 'hood," I admit it to her, words I would never confess to anyone else.

"Son, tell Mama Vee what's going on." She stops fiddling with the supplies and settles onto the high stool she teaches from. She points to a chair. "Sit down and talk to me. I aint a gossip, and it seems like you need an ear."

"This school… it aint like the ones here. I jai like feel that nothing I do is considered worthy of respect." The truth rolls out from me and I can't stop. Ms. Yashar and her steady disrespect – her daily attacks on my intelligence, my actions, my worth. The cliquish students who've long before chosen their inner-circles and have no room for new recruits. The hallways filled with fashion labels and flashes of cash; they aint exactly welcoming the 'hood transplant in my plain tee and jeans. "I wouldn't normally care about being ignored. Get in where I fit in, ya know? But if Teach aint feeling me – if she makes it impossible to succeed in her class – I'm not gonna make it to New York. Hell, I aint gonna make my graduation."

"Language," she chastises gruffly. "And you *will* graduate, Tru. There is no other option. What's your mama saying about the class? I know Miss Pitre isn't accepting this... what did you say her name was?"

"Ms. Yashar."

"Uh huh. Your mama aint gonna let some snooty teacher swindle her son's grade or squander his future," she's looking me straight in the eyes and I gotta keep from squirming under the scrutiny. "Hmmm. You aint tell her?"

Mama Vee knows me all too well. I shake my head and stare at the floor. If I look her in the eyes – 'cause I know she is still looking right at me – I might lose it.

"I see. Let me call Stephani. Unacceptable, Tru. I've taught you better than this. Advocate – for yourself and for those who can't." She's already dialing Ma on her phone.

"I'm gonna go to the bathroom before the kids come in, Mama Vee," I say standing and walking to the door. She shoos me along with a wave.

"Hello Stephani," she's connected to Ma as I dip out.

I make my way to the restroom and then it dawns on me that I'm not safe here anymore. Too many new folk are rolling into the center and I'm not here enough now to know 'em all. I check the stalls for occupants, pounding my fist into the door of each one to open it. The restroom is empty. Exhale.

Back in the art room, Mama Vee is greeting her students. "Yes, baby, this is your piece of our mural," she says to one boy of about ten. He's looking at her through dreads that hang across his forehead and over his eyes. "Tru, you take a plank, too. I want you to add to our wall, as well." She's smiling at me, and this time it's genuine. I guess the convo with Ma went well.

But I still gotta inquire about what she's heard and what that means for my time at the rec center. Can't do it in front of the kids, so I'm gonna have to ask when class is over.

***

Mama Vee excuses herself from the center right after class. "Ron, I need to get Tru to the station, class cleanup ran long and I don't want him to miss his train home."

"Yes, ma'am," Ron answers, looking up from his mopping. He's been a janitor here for as long as I can remember. He also coaches a kickball league for the peewee players. "I'll lock up."

Inside her beat up little car, which grunts and grinds as she shifts into gear, Mama Vee finally decides to give it to me straight. "Tru, these thugs been coming into the rec more often now. I know you didn't tell your Ma about that encounter with Erik. I don't think you called your P-O either."

"Mama, I don't talk to Ma too often about things that're gonna stress her. She's workin' mad hours 'cause of me and I aint tryna add to her worry. As it is, she's gonna be sleep on the couch when I get in waitin' for me to return safe."

"I see. Stephani paying all your restitution herself?"

"Yes."

"Lord'ave mercy. Look, you gonna do these hours like we planned, but you aren't gonna be able to just stroll down the street to the rec center anymore. I don't know what was so sweet about the Nicolas girls, but Erik seems to think you did more than move his lady out of the neighborhood."

"What? I..."

"I know, Tru. We're gonna get you out of this case, out of high school and off to university." She pulls up to the station's Kiss and Ride drop off and turns toward me. "You gotta talk to your mother about school – that's on you. But I'll handle the rec and you'll get your service."

"You didn't tell her?"

"You're man enough now to speak for yourself, chile. Go on, get." She shoos me out of the car.

I glance back at her as I'm walking up the stairs to the train platform. She's still idling in her car, watching me, so I wave. She salutes me and revs her engine, which coughs and sputters in response before she pulls off from the curve.

Erik isn't going away. I get it now. The doors close on the train as I settle into a seat for the ride home.

***

One term separates me from graduation. One: the longest I've ever experienced.

I've been doing a little snooping on Ms. Yashar. Ever since Teach had that afterschool sob session, she's either tried to ignore my existence entirely by avoiding eye contact and proximity, or she's nit-picked on anything and everything I do or *don't*. I've huffed or sighed or breathed too loud in silent reading. Uh, okay. I've moved too slow to my group – except my desk is usually where e'ryone assembles, sliding theirs up against mine for our literary discussions. Though my hand is always raised to answer her questions and *try* to demonstrate my intelligence, she looks right around me and calls on another student every time. She even called on a kid who leans against the wall looking like he's enjoying the flight, his glazed eyes failing to focus and hide his obvious high. And when he could only respond "wha--- uh, well... I'm not sure... can I get back to you?"

She merely nodded and said, "Yes, take some time to think about it."

I can't lie, I'm shocked she was so accommodating. If it'd been me with no answer...

Ms. Yashar is finally grading my written work. I had to get my Ma involved. Imagine a senior having his mama complain about an unreasonable teacher requirement. Travesty.

Ma, who was sitting comfortably on our couch, requested a phone conversation. It went like this (from Ma's side, of course):

"Yes. It's nice to speak to you also, Ms. Yashar. ... No. This is not a social call, ma'am. ... am I to understand you refuse to read printed work? ... Why?"

Ma stood at this point, sometimes leaning her weight on the arm rest, then pacing as she spoke and stopping to focus on Ms. Yashar's reply.

"... And what was the goal of the assignment? ... I see. So there is no reason for the online component other than to streamline *your* work? ... I'm sorry? ... no. I do *not* see the point here. Is this not an English class? If his work is done, legibly – typed even .... Are you saying it is not? ... Uh huh. That's what I thought. So you *will* be reviewing his assignments, then? ... Yes, of course ... Thank you. We will be in touch again."

I could speculate about Teach's retorts – about how Ma had her stammering for a real justification for not assessing my work. Ms. Yashar touts this 'new age classroom' belief about how responding online is going to prepare us for the future of communication across the globe. Maybe there is a lot of through- the- net correspondence; sending an email is faster than snail mail (especially when I can never find stamps where they're supposed to be). But you gotta be able to write something first, right?

Ma don't play about school – or anything else. And she aint sharing my business any more than absolutely necessary. I don't know what story she told admin to enroll me. Pro'lly didn't tell them anything; just showed the lease verifying we live in the district and passed my transcript across the table. That's how she *said* she was handling it. No reason to divulge details about my court concerns that don't concern this school. Or the college. Or anyone else.

So my 4-1-1 is under wraps unless I choose to unwrap it. I aint choosin' to.

Anyway, I did a little recon on Teach. I figure it's her personality to make assumptions about people. But I aint the one to assume anything about somebody's character, so I gotta do my research and observation.

First thing I noticed is the dark rectangular spot on the colored paper covering the bulletin board. That paper fades so much during the year even if this classroom keeps the blinds to the windows closed most days, so it's obvious when someone changes out the postings. This darkness is about the size of a 5x7 photo and there's remnants of tape in the two upper corners. Too small to be an office memo, or an inspiring quote – and she's got a lot of 'em around the room printed large for motivation.

She took off her ring. I wouldn't have noticed except she slammed her left hand on my desk yesterday when I was reading. I was supposed to be composing some response to her journal prompt, which I'd done quickly, as I usually do. I dunno how she expected me to fill my spare time, and reading – in previous English classes – was encouraged.

"Tru!" she shouted as her hand connected with the desk. "Why aren't you working on your journal?"

"Finished."

She stood there waiting for the proof of my statement, so I marked the page in my book and flipped through the notebook to my required response. She scrutinized the page, no doubt looking for something to criticize, but finding the length more than she'd required and the content – which she seemed to skim – satisfactory, she crossed her arms and click-clacked across the room to her desk without another word to me.

I saw it, though, in that brief exchange. Her ring finger was pale and slightly indented where a ring used to be. I'd never noticed what she once wore there, but it is definitely gone now.

In the trashcan the other day, I noticed a number of discarded envelops – the kind in various shades of bright colors warning of urgency before the final notices come. I didn't pick through the rubbish, but it was clear that there was more than one collector waiting on their payment. I can't say why Ms. Yashar would empty her bag into this kinda public place; but this can is as good as any other when you know garbage is gonna pile up on top of it. And it is *her* classroom.

Sometimes the reflection of her computer screen is visible in the window behind her. All that clicking she does? Shopping. I think Teach therapy-shops, if that's a thing. That'd explain the parade of shoes and clothes that are rarely repeated. Some teachers have an unofficial uniform they wear to school every day - regularly reappearing skirts or pants or shirts - but not her.

I've seen her fervently typing, too. At first I thought she was reviewing the digital class assignments or some such, but now I think she is browsing through websites for information. It's not an aimless search, either. She's looking for something specific – scrutinizing the results, scrolling with the mouse and angrily tapping the keyboard.

I can't pinpoint why she was so upset the other day, but – and I'm really speculating with this inference like she tells us to do with our readings – Ms. Yashar is pro'lly newly single and the breakup with her spouse is anything but amicable.

Aint no wonder she is frustrated with life. It isn't me. It isn't even this at-capacity class. She might really be in dire financial straits and her personal life is unraveling.

I wish she'd figure all that out, though, cause she's straight oblivious to what's happening in her class. Does she realize how she treats people? Or that the students in her class got issues? No. She doesn't - or she doesn't care because she's hung up with her own concerns.

Pom Pom Posse controls the social scene. Parties, shopping trips, "vay-kays" – bougie for vacations – they're behind them, in the midst of them, or crushing them on a whim for not being P-3 *approved*. Clearly I aint a part of the P-3's circle. They're not gonna dap me up as we pass. Can't text me an invite. No one gonna hit me up in class about chillin' afterschool. P-3 don't know me.

It's pro'lly a good thing. I jai like anonymity. Saves me from snoops and snitches, no one knows where I'm from or where I'm going.

Not too many caramel or chocolate folk here – especially not sistas. No, I'm not tryna find me a girl (and her pigment doesn't mean a thing, anyway), but I can look. When I first started attending here, one or two of these girls grabbed their purses like I'd've stolen from 'em in the middle of class as I pass to my desk. They got me marked a thug just by skin alone.

People always pass judgement and their true colors looking darker than mine. I can speak eloquently should the occasion need me to do so. And I write with a "clarity well beyond my years" – insert air quotes – Mr. Logan always said that about my work at my old school. But these people take one look at me in my oversized shirt and baggy jeans, with my hair twisted and dyed, and my brown skin and I'm someone of whom to be wary.

No matter how I approach the situation, I stand out even when I try to blend into the background. I'm either the first encounter with a person of color or being linked to every prior encounter with one. It's a hefty responsibility being the representative of melanated skin. Every comment I make, every grade recorded, every intonation of my voice or expression on my face becomes the "standard" reference.

Maybe that's why my nearly perfected Charlie is my go-to for self-amusement. Or is it preservation? Can't say that this black dude was rude or sketchy if all they know is my Chaplin comedy skits. If every time Teach is on my case, I react with humor - with exaggerated gestures and (my personal favorite) the slew-footed scuttle around my desk – I'll keep my good vibes only status.

And the dudes at this school? I can deal with them all: athletes, scholars, musicians, performers, the lost, the enlightened, the mute.

One stands out - Zeke is my man. He schooled me on "whom to befriend" and "whom to avoid." He talks funny proper like that when there aren't any listening ears save my own. But if he's got an audience? It's like his speech is a mad lib for slang: insert flava here. I wonder how many of the peeps in class know his father is a Baptist preacher and mother is a lawyer? His front is solid, so I doubt anyone would suspect the extent of his class act.

Nell's been the biggest shock in all this – not because I assumed anything about her but because she is so unapologetically open. About her bum parents. About her desperation to escape the family home. About not fitting in – her on purpose unapproachability – so as not to need to talk about anything.

Nell

At the end of class, Tru stood quickly. He walked over to Nell's desk, one hand buried in the bag he carried. He fished inside it and pulled out a few VHS tapes tied together with a shoelace.

"For you," he said, waving his hand and bending at his waist as though mimicking the beginnings of an elaborate royal bow. "On loan, of course. They're my favorites."

She studied the tapes. "I… uh… how am I supposed to watch them?"

Tru was momentarily shocked. His brows furrowed, then he laughed. "I hadn't thought about that."

"Tru, I've not seen a VHS player since… well, since watching throwback movies on streaming video. Every eighties and nineties classroom seemed to come with those rolling TV stands with the player on the lower shelf."

"Uh, yeah, I feel ya." He shrugged, seemingly unphased.

"I could…" she paused, reconsidering whether she should volunteer a visit to his home. Would he think it intrusive? No, hadn't he said that watching the videos was important to showing her his inspirations? Surely he'd want to facilitate that. "I could come by your place, maybe? I mean, we could ask the librarians downtown if they still have a system set up, but…"

"Naw."

"No?"

"I mean, yeah, you can come over. Le'me clear it with Ma – check her sched' to make sure we aren't interrupting her sleep time. She's grinding mad hours."

"She's what?"

"Working. All the time. Money's tight, ya'know?"

Nell nodded automatically. Tru wasn't typical. She couldn't imagine anyone else in their class mentioning financial limitations – or any hardship, really. They were all too busy flashing the latest and greatest tech, or the season's newest released clothes and shoes. The school's student parking lot was full of new cars, especially as graduation drew closer.

But Tru? If he wasn't the first in the classroom in the morning, he arrived just before the tardy bell huffing as though he had trekked a long way to get there – certainly more spent than someone who had merely walked from his car to the building. And he'd met her at the library coming from the direction of the public transit. He didn't have a cell phone. No smart watch. Just white tee, denim, well-worn sneakers, a nondescript backpack, and the copy of Tupac Shakur's book he'd gotten from his friend, Jo.

How *different* life must be for Tru. *And how privileged am I?*

***

Their three-week deadline was a third wasted. But true to his word, Tru had cleared his schedule with his mother. The next morning, he walked to her desk.

"We set for this evening, if you don't already have plans."

"Plans? Ha!" Nell was surprised he'd even suggested it. "You should know by now my plans consist of school, home, and whatever ride I can stretch out in between to stay out of said home."

"Word. I feel you."

Tru tore a piece of loose leaf in half and jotted his address on it. He folded it over on itself twice before handing it to Nell. "Me," he said as she took the note and slide it into her satchel.

"I'll be over at four, if that's okay with you?"

"Yeah. Ma will be workin' a double, so we won't disturb her. Though these days, she sleeps so heavily that she wouldn't hear the movies playing, anyway." His face clouded with sadness for a moment as he spoke.

Nell asked gently, whispering, "How much more do you owe?"

Tru closed his eyes, doing a mental calculation. "Pro'lly about five or six grand still. I know it don't seem like much, but on top of the crib, transport and food? It might as well be a mil."

Nell wasn't sure how to respond. She nodded, allowing an awkward silence to settle between them.

Suddenly, an ear-piercing scream jolted them both from their thought.

"Oh-emm-gee! Claire, Sue, look!" it was Carrie, clutching her cell phone tightly as she held it at arm's length in front of her, her knuckles white with the grip's intensity. Her eyes, wide with what seemed like shock, were glassy and then the tears stated. Her chest heaved as she ugly cried.

Sue and Claire took their time to reach their friend. Claire perched on the desk and reached for the extended phone. She casually glanced at the screen. Sue stood next to her, one hand covering her mouth, the other reaching across Claire's arm as she dragged her finger across the screen to advance its image.

As the crying intensified, others who had been equally stunned by the outburst stared at the scene unfolding before them. Ms. Yashar looked up initially shocked by the volume of Carrie's wale, but had apparently decided it was not worth the effort to quiet her down or interfere in the girl crisis playing out in her class.

Nell glanced toward the girls in curiosity, but quickly looked away. She'd learned early on that involving herself in their issues invited them to turn their attention toward her — a sort of projection of attitude Nell wasn't interested in entertaining.

The dismissal bell sounded then and the hallway cacophony drowned out the sobbing and chatter inside Ms. Yashar's room.

"A'ight, Nell," Tru, disinterested in the climaxing drama, said. "See you at four."

He walked briskly out of class.

During last block government, while the documentary on grassroots campaigning dragged on, Nell unfolded Tru's note. She looked at the address he'd written —

693 Low Knole St, Lower

She'd never seen "lower" on an address. Was that another word for apartment? The mapping program on her phone didn't offer any clarification. In fact, the street view image showed a set of rowhouses, which she knew were single family dwellings. *He really needs a cell phone. What if I get lost?*

Nell didn't need to worry. As she pulled her car up to the curb in front of the houses, Tru was waiting on the concrete stoop of 693. He walked toward her as she turned off the ignition and grabbed her satchel.

"Aren't you prompt," he teased as he opened her door for her.

"And you are quite the gentleman, Tru."

"Surprised? Ma didn't raise no rude boy."

"I see."

He closed her door after she stepped out and led her onto the property, but he did not return to the steps leading to the door. Instead, he walked around the perimeter of the house to a metal fence.

"My entrance is back here," he assured her. "I probably should've mentioned that. Ours is the basement of this one."

He unlocked the back-door screen and pushed open the heavy wooden storm door. "Welcome to Casa del Pitre." Another flourishing royal bow, which Nell knew was one of his favorite (and most endearing) moves.

Inside, Nell noticed the staircase leading up to a padlocked door. The apartment was a converted basement of the brownstone. The homeowners must've wanted it to look larger than it was, using bright white paint on every wall. Even the counters of the modest kitchen were white. The small living room was sparsely decorated. She noticed a few pictures of Tru at various ages, some with a lovely light skinned woman she guessed was his mom who wore her hair in two braids that rested on her shoulders. The framed photos sat on a bookshelf positioned next to a plush couch that seemed far too large for the space. The dining area had a small circular table and two matching wooden chairs, large seat cushions tied securely to their slated backs. The table was set with black placemats and cloth napkins rolled and held by copper circles. Against the wall was a computer sitting on a folding table; its keyboard covered by envelops. There was no TV in the room they had entered.

"So..." Nell had stopped just inside the door, waiting for further invitation.

"Oh, damn. The telly's in the room here. If that makes you uncomfortable, it'll just take a minute to move it out here?"

"No. No that won't be necessary, Tru." She smiled, hoping it'd reassure him. She wasn't at all uncomfortable in his home. He'd given her no reason to doubt his intentions were anything but to watch the movies he'd insisted she see. *People always assume the worst, don't they?*

"I'll keep the door open. Ma'll be home about eight unless she picks up another shift." He walked to the room and popped the first tape into the VHS system. "Showtime!"

Nell followed him in and settled onto the only surface available besides the floor – the bed. While he was adjusting the old television set's volume, she chanced scanning the space. Tru's room walls were bare. A calendar was attached to the closet with a thumb tack, several dates had figures written neatly in the corners and others said "rec" or "court" or "check-in." A two shelf book case held several paperbacks. Tru's beloved Tupac book was sitting on the top. Taped to the side of the bookshelf was a Polaroid of a young girl with long curly hair hugging Tru around his shoulders, in his hand was a video camera. They looked like they were laughing. *That must be Jo*, Nell thought, but she didn't dare ask to confirm.

Tru plopped down onto the floor, leaning against the bed.

For several hours they watched the VHS tapes Tru had determined were primaries for film. He got up from the floor once or twice, stretching awkwardly.

"You okay?"

"Butts asleep. Legs are, too." He smiled at her as he rubbed his backside and massaged his legs.

"You can join me here, if it'd be more comfortable? It is your room, Tru." She patted a space on the bed next to her, but Tru shook his head vehemently.

"Naw. Respect, though." He smiled.

It was rare that Nell dealt with someone so keenly aware of boundaries and personal space. She returned the smile. "Always."

Tru

When Nell was over my place yesterday, she was more relaxed than I'd ever seen her. I mean, she aint never been uncomfortable around me, or anyone that I'd seen. It's more like she's build a wall to surround herself and keep out the world. But yesterday? Her partition cracked a bit and it didn't seem like she was tasting her words before she spoke to determine how the flavor would be received.

I know she comes from money. She drives a nice car. She has a fancy bike. She sketches in a moleskin notebook with those old school nibs and an ink bottle – which, by the way, she was real bold to have set on the edge of her desk in class with the top off. The mess that'd make if it fell! Art supplies are loaded into her leather satchel. She went through most of them, holding out her gold leaf origami papers, color pencils she keeps in a rolled bundle, a set of black drawing pencils (who knew there was more than #2?) and a white roll paper she called a tortillon. The only disparity is her wardrobe. I can't quite figure out the style she's working, but designer label clothes are not her thing.

Despite all she has, she's not pretentious at all. She walked into our little apartment without so much as a glance at the tiny

"

accommodations. She didn't even hesitate when I pointed to the bedroom where my TV-VCR is set up. She plopped onto the bed and shucked her shoes to the floor like she was family.

Anyway, today she hands me her moleskin and says, "I think I've got it."

And I'm thinking, *yeah right* until I look at the page she's flipped to, full of notes for our project.

Damn Nell, have you done this before?

TEXT TITLE: Acceptable Me — My truth, without consequence

[Should this be a voice over, also?]

Camera shot on an androgynous person.

Face is covered by blank mask - no features painted on.

Clothing is unisex, plain.

Pull back from close-up to show several similarly attired, gender unidentifiable people.

These are minions of life.

Color scheme is drab. [Should this be Black & White??]

Yes! Then it's not about ethnicity.

Image distortion - Can we do a scramble like old cable with weak signal? How would this look?

Switch to color? Start as a glowing light, maybe, from main person's heart? Then expand?

It is symbolic of the colorful person inside, begging to be free.

When camera pans up, can the mask be removed? A sort of reveal of the true self.

Is main person's face masculine?

Maybe he has smeared makeup, but it's reversed like he tries to be a "normal" guy, but under the façade it is more decorated?

The screen flashes to several vignettes of stereotypes -- maybe film someone flipping through magazine images of masculinity? Would this violate someone's copyright?

VOICE OVER: You want a manly man. You beat me down with words to conform me. Inside
I scream. I am me! What happened to respect. Don't you love me for who I am? I am
becoming. I have become. Your words cut...

Flash to illustration? One of bare arms, the wrists scarred from cutting.

VOICE OVER: Your words numb my spirit. Sometimes I cut to feel. But it doesn't make me
feel better. It isn't healthy. Sometimes I have remind myself of myself.

Show mirror. Show man from initial scene looking at Reflection of man in tailored suit
jacket, pencil skirt. [Like Aidan's?] He is happy.

Photos of first man with people. Maybe a series of casual dates? Restaurant scene.
Show date, then quick flashing of man's face. Only happy with one, straight-faced
or sad with others.

VOICE OVER shouting: Be a man! I didn't raise *this*. You are **dead** to me.

Black screen, at least 2 seconds of nothing.

Then, man speaks: I'm alive when I am me.

Should stats go here? Do we really need them?

VOICE OVER and screen text: your understanding isn't needed, but your acceptance is.

Maybe a gradient of the pride colors? No, a flash of the flags ending on the ally flag.

A scrolling of key hashtags:

> #stopthebullying #trueidentity #realme #supporteachother #pride

When I glance up, she's looking over the notebook, too. I'm
nodding and she is smiling as together we review her notes.

"Do'ya like?" she says it quiet, like she isn't confident, but her smile
has broadened, and her eyes are wide as she anticipates my approval.

"It's... wow. This is solid."

"Can we do it? Is it too much?"

"I'm'a have to talk to someone about editing software, but yeah. I
know exactly how we can get this on point."

"Wait - - editing software. I forgot... is it gonna interfere with
your..."

"Naw." I wasn't sure who might be listening to the exchange, so I cut her off quick. My parole officer might need to approve the computer I'm on, but it's easy enough to block the 'net while I'm piecing together our spot.

What Nell's envisioned is golden. Inspired, even. Aint no way this script could fail us.

***

Suddenly I see the parallels between this script and me. I been clowning so long in class that no one in this place knows the true Tru. I don't know that I *want* to share myself — I rather like the masked identity. But here is Nell, who has had years of these people scrutinizing her and she has neither crumbled nor changed. She is Nell — the artist, the emotionally charged, the reticent. There's more passion in that sketchbook of hers than some of our classmates have found in the entirety of their shallow lives. And she doesn't seem phased much by what anyone thinks.

I jai like envy Nell.

Nell

Nell unlocked the door to her house and stepped inside. Quietly setting her keys on the table in the foyer, she slid off her shoes and walked sock-footed towards the kitchen for a glass of orange juice.

She poured herself a large glass and was closing the fridge as the muffled voices of her parents intensified to shouting.

"How dare you, Andreas! Nothing is *ever* your fault."

"You've got that right. You let him parade around in women's clothing. It's harmless, you said. Let him *express himself*. And he kept right on."

"He was your son!"

"Son? Son? Ha!" A door slammed in the hallway. "My son played little league. He did not wear pumps and skirts and bring his boyfriend home to dinner!"

"My baby is dead!" Her voice was shrill and loud – nearing hysterics.

"If you'd stopped babying him, he'd have been a man."

Mrs. Necahaul was crying, then.

Nell had heard this fight before. Her parents arguing over who "made" Aidan the man he had become. *There was no one to blame for Aidan being himself.*

They were, however, both to blame for what happened to their family. Her mother hadn't stopped Aidan from leaving. Mrs. Necahaul didn't visit him in the home he shared with Chay – not once. It may have been Nell's father who pointed to the door, but it was her mother who stood silent as he walked out.

Nell quickly gulped down her orange juice, then washed the glass and set in on the towel next to the sink. She walked swiftly and quietly to the stairs, careful to avoid making noise that might alert her parents to her presence in the house. In her room with her door closed, she lay on her bed with her scrapbook. She felt like crying, the lump in her throat making it hard to swallow. But her tears failed her. She flipped open the book, tracing the edge of the page she landed on with her finger as she looked at the family photo carefully affixed to the crisp ivory paper. There were a lot of these photos – part of the family tradition of picture cards - one for every Christmas, one for each Easter. They stopped abruptly, leaving blank pages at the back of the book where more documenting portraits should have resided.

***

It was a week before Easter. Then, Aidan was a junior in high school. Their mother had carefully curated their clothes to match the year's color scheme based on the swatches released by Pantone. She was meticulous about selecting outfits that coordinated without being exact replicas of each other. Sometimes it took her weeks to compose "the look" for the portrait session. Then, when she was satisfied with each costume, the clothes were pressed and set in each respective room.

"Be dressed and ready by 10 sharp," their father had said the morning of their appointment.

But it was already 10:12 as Nell sat in the foyer on the settee, buckling her dress shoes. Mr. Necahaul stood impatiently, looking at his watch and tapping his foot on the wood floor.

Mrs. Necahaul walked to the base of the staircase as she fixed her earring, and called upstairs, "Aidan? Let's hurry it up, okay?"

"Coming." Nell noticed his voice sounded odd.

"We'll be outside," Mr. Necahaul said, ushering Nell toward the door. They waited in the car for Aidan.

At twenty-two past ten, he walked out the family home, closing and locking the door before walking down the driveway. Aidan walked deliberately slow toward the idling car but not in the outfit their mother had chosen. He'd traded the slacks for a pencil skirt and wrapped the required necktie around his button-down shirt at the waist.

"What the h-" Mr. Necahaul began as Aidan got close to his open window.

"I made some adjustments, dad."

"Where are the clothes I laid out for you?" Mrs. Necahaul said, her voice a mixture of nervousness and exasperation. She was watching her husband carefully.

"I like this better. It matches your scheme, right?" He swept his hands down in front his body showing off the look. Nell took note of Aidan's outfit which did, actually, match everyone else's attire.

"Get in." Mr. Necahaul said through clenched teeth. He was seething. "I've already paid the photographer a retainer."

Aidan, face set to blank expression, climbed into the car and buckled his seatbelt.

When they arrived at the park for their photo session, the photographer carefully positioned Aidan behind Nell so that his outfit was barely visible. They shot a few seated photos. Then, when it was time for the "kid's portrait," Mr. Necahaul refused to allow Aidan to pose unless he and Nell were captured from waist up. The photographer tried to oblige.

Back home, Nell covered her head with her pillow to muffle the yelling outside her room.

The next morning, Nell knocked timidly on Aidan's door. He answered after some time, his eyes puffy and hair unkempt.

She waited until she was invited inside his room and the door was closed, to ask. "Why do you push Dad's buttons like that?"

"Girl, you know," he smiled weakly. "I gotta be me. If I can't be who I want to be at home – with my family – how can I be myself in the street? Clothes don't have a gender. Besides, I looked fab-u-lous in that skirt, didn't I."

Nell giggled. "Well, yeah. But I think you could've left off the tie."

When the finished portraits arrived, tensions rose in the house again. Mr. Necahaul raged for several days, and Mrs. Necahaul banished Aidan to his room. The photos were placed in a drawer, the space for the biannual portrait left empty in the scrapbook. They didn't schedule family photos for Christmas that year.

***

Little sticky notes and old receipts with messages were pressed inside other pages. Aidan left them in Nell's backpack or between the pages of her notebooks and textbooks. "Inspirations" he called them.

She flipped to the back of the scrapbook and peeled back the clingy film holding the page's contents in place. Behind a birthday card she'd stashed a photo of Aidan and Chay. On the back, he'd written "Our First Thanksgiving" - the one he'd wanted to share with the family. Nell replaced the picture under the card, resealed the page, and closed the book.

She pulled her moleskin from her satchel and started sketching – this time an image of her brother and his beau.

She'd have to take Tru to visit with Chay. He'd be perfect as the voice over artist. And, she decided, he would read the statistics currently missing in their video outline. Tomorrow, she'd look up the most recent reports from "The Trevor Project," an organization Aidan and Chay had been active in. Aidan had said they'd helped him when he was an uncertain teen. According to their website, they'd become "the leading national organization providing crisis intervention and suicide prevention services to lesbian, gay, bisexual, transgender, queer & questioning youth."

After school the next day, Nell met up with Tru in the student parking lot. She'd brought her car so they could ride together to Chay's house.

Chay was surprised when she'd called to ask to come over. "Are you sure, Nell-Belle? Didn't your dad flip out the last time he tracked you here?"

"Yeah, he did. But I need your help with something important. And now I know to turn off the phone when I'm out and about."

Tru agreed to solicit help without hesitation. "This is great. I mean, we got that theatre student to play our lead, but if Chay will be our voice over for part of the piece, it'll fit just right."

Chay greeted them at the door and ushered them inside the home that he and Aidan had shared. The walls were covered in photographs – mostly of architecture, but there were also pictures of the couple.

Following Tru's gaze to the pictures, Chay offered, "Aidan took all of those – except the portraits of us. He had an eye for capturing beauty in the industrial spaces around town."

"I'm jai like looking at an art gallery, man."

Chay smiled proudly. "Yeah. Talent runs in the family. Nell mentioned you're going to school next year for film?"

"If it all falls into place. Got a few loose ends to seal and then I'm good."

"Graduation?"

"On the horizon," Nell interjected. "If we can get this PSA done, Ms. Yashar's English class is *finito*."

Something in the way she said the teacher's name alerted Chay. "I take it we don't like her?"

"She's got issues," Tru said. He didn't bother to elaborate.

Chay nodded. "Who doesn't?"

"And a grudge against Tru that is unreal and unfair," Nell added.

"I see. So how can I help you two, Nelly?" He was fiddling with his wedding ring – a gold band with "A and C" engraved into it.

Tru offered him Nell's drafted script and waited as Chay read through it.

"We've got a great actor doing the pantomimes. But we need a deeper voice, like yours, as the authority. If you could be the voice of our video, it'd be golden."

Nell walked him through their ideas. She explained, "Aidan wanted nothing more than to live his truth. This is what this PSA is about."

Nodding, Chay smiled. "I'm sold. When do we start?"

Streets are dead tonight. The usual foot traffic past my post on the corner aint passin' though and I'm wondering if the block is hot. E'ry so often, cops hype up patrols, keeping hood folk on high alert from the increased presence. Police like Peeping Toms watching our comings and goings, taking notes on who is doing what and where they're doing it. Most of the officers just drive through real slow, scanning the streets for suspicious activity – or for thugs lurking in the shadows of the alleys.

Foot patrol don't come through at night. They'd be more effective, though, 'cause the headlights from the patrol cars have hustlers scattering like roaches fleeing the kitchen light suddenly turning on.

They aint really tryna mess wit' me, pro'ly 'cause I'm conspicuous under the glow of the street light. No one doing dirt – exhibiting illicit behavior, as they say – does it in the open. 'Xcept me. I'm into being bold and shit.

The boy is late tonight. I saw him heading toward the rec last week around this time, coming from the train station. He was walking like he found some brand new happy – hands shoved in his jacket pockets, hood pulled over his head, damn near skipping along the sidewalk – I guess he forgot he owes me an explanation.

No one gets to interrupt my bi'nez. And him? He invaded my harem and sent my girls off. Don't he know my property is *mine*?

It's been a few months since my girl packed up her life and she and her kid disappeared. It didn't take her long, either. I came back from a quick pick up to an open door, all the lights in the apartment on. Conspicuous as hell that something wasn't right. Aint no one answer when I called out from the hallway. No one in the place. Living room looked like it always did, TV blasting and Jo's school books stacked on the corner of the coffee table. Smells of dinner wafted from the covered pots and pans on the stove. But my girl and her kid wasn't no where to be found.

Texted her. When she didn't hit me back quick like she always did, I called her. Her phone went straight to voicemail. She knows better than to miss my call. Then I saw them – sitting on the kitchen counter – her keys.

What the hell was going on?

Kids room was clean – bed made up with stuffed animals laying on the pillows, except the picture frames on her night stand were empty. And her closet? There, empty hangers littered the floor. Her shoes were there, laying neatly in pairs along the bottom, but her clothes were cleared out.

Shit was embarrassing as hell, asking around for my woman and the kid. No one knew where they were. Streets were unusually quiet.

Then the 'hood's talking about some wiz kid being tried for larceny. Seems like he swindled some companies outta quite a bit of money. Newspapers hushed from name dropping – juvenile orders or somethin' – but street sources say it's Stephani's kid, Tru. The same boy who aint stopped through to check on his girl Jo since she took off. Aint no coincidence that he and his mama disappear soon after.

Imagine my surprise seeing him again, walking to the rec like he aint been MIA for months. So I step to him for a chat and he pales like he's seeing a ghost. Cat's eyes darting all around like he tryna find an escape route.

I let him leave – customers take priority over personal bi'nez. Besides, if he so bold to be back at the rec, I knew I could find him again.

Now tonight is the night he's usually moving this way and I aint seen Tru nowhere.

Caught him at the station just as his train rolled out. I know he saw me, too. But it aint over. My boys will find him so we can discuss some things.

Meanwhile it's bi'nez as usual. Gotta keep my ends tight and my rep right.

Tru

The train ride to the rec has always been my oasis. I know for most people who commute on public transit that the rocking of the cars along the track and the crowds of people unintentionally encroaching on personal space is cringe-worthy. But for me, with my headphones in my ears and my shades on, the train gives me time to think and observe. I could ride for hours – to the end of the line and back – just watching the passenger interactions.

Ever since the brief encounter with Erik, though, my ride into the old 'hood has been filled with apprehension. I'm not looking for another run-in with dude and now that he knows I'm around still, I'm pretty sure he's set up shop closer to the path he knows I tread.

Mama Vee has a way of getting information out of me. Her prodding about my "mood change" lasted the entirety of my shift. So I told her that I'd talked to Erik. Then, when Erik's flunkies started hanging out in the rec center and my name became abuzz, she promptly changed my schedule.

There's only one route from the station, so I walk it on high alert. I scan the streets in front of me and listen to the sounds around me. In the warmer days of late May, the kids are outside. Teens are staring at cell phones huddled in groups, but the younger kids are riding bikes, playing hopscotch on the sidewalks or double-dutch in the street. Their mamas are usually nearby, 'cause it aint safe to let them get further than shouting distance away.

Tonight, I'm supposed to report to the rec by 6pm. It's still light out when I step off the train and head to work. It's crazy hot today, so I'm gonna stop at the corner store on my way. It's just down the block a bit and across the street.

When I was little, the shop's owner used to keep loose candy on the counter for kids to purchase with a few coins. He made more profit with the nickel and dime sweets than with the higher priced bags of candy we could hardly afford. On days when the temperatures climaxed and the sweltering heat took over, he'd put out ice cold water in a cooler for the passersby. Ownership changed, though, and the new proprietors aren't interested in continuing the traditions.

There's a slender lady standing out front in a short dress, sipping something from a paper bag. Her bangles jingle on her wrists as she raises and lowers her drink.

"Hey suga," she says as I walk past her to get through the door she's now holding open.

I nod and smile, but do not reply. I don't have anything she wants and she's got nothing I need.

Scanning the fridge at the back of the store, I locate a juice and take it to the counter.

The door chimes as it opens and closes behind another customer. I can't see who has come in, but I hear him as he talks into his phone. Erik.

"Keep the change." I gotta get outta this store.

The door chimes as I open it and he turns.

"Tru - -"

I'm almost running to the rec as he calls after me.

"We got *bih*-nezz to discuss Tru!"

Mama Vee is outside talking to a lady who's been a regular at the rec center since I was little. Mama's holding the lady's little boy in her arms, swaying as she "loves him up," kissing his cheeks and hugging him. The boy's mother is smiling.

"I loves me some Quint-on!" she's nearly singing. "You love Mama Vee, right?"

"Yes!" the boy's lisp slurs his cheery reply.

I keep on toward the rec door, "Hi Mama Vee! Hi Miss Queen, Quinton."

"Tru baby, what's the hurry?" Mama's voice follows me. She'll no doubt be hustling inside herself.

I'm sitting on the bleachers of the gym, trying to focus on the two-on-two game in front of me. The industrial blowers of the air conditioner are on blast, but I'm still sweating. Shaking the collar of my shirt isn't helping me. I feel like I'm suffocating.

Erik isn't going to stop coming for me until I talk to him. I got nothing to say. Don't know where Jo and Ma Nicolas went with the money. And all this – the move, dealing with Teach, Ma working until she drops from exhaustion – would be for nothing if I did know and could lead him right to them. He thinks he owns "his girls" and I've interfered with his property possession.

"Tru?" It's Mama Vee, of course. She's stood in front of me so I have to focus on her. "I'm done with this, baby. You aint fixin' to be running for your life every time you come for these hours. If you don't call your PO, I will."

"Mama, I aint no snitch."

"No, you're not. But Erik isn't gonna squash his vendetta against you if he thinks you're hiding something of his."

"But - -"

"No. I'm not gonna wait to see you hurt. Or killed." Arguing against that is futile. She lost her son to these streets.

I nod. She is right. I could try to avoid Erik and risk a run in, or I could... no. He hadn't done anything to me. All the PO can do is change my community service assignment. This here is my community even if I aint livin' in it right now. This is the 'hood that raised me. But I can't tell Mama Vee this. She has to be assured I'm going to have the PO watching out for my safety.

"A'ight."

"You can use my phone." She points to the doors and I've got no choice but to walk toward her office. She doesn't have to know I'm not going to call.

Nell

Nell never did talk to Ms. Yashar about Tru. She knew there was a reason he wasn't candid about his predicament – especially since not talking about his restrictions was such a source of strife in the classroom. No one would risk failing while doing all the work if it wasn't serious, Ms. Yashar had to know that. But the fact that she didn't seem interested in inquiring for herself about Tru's adamant refusal to use the digital classroom was testament to her dislike for him. Armed with information about his conviction, she might make trouble for him.

So Nell couldn't help him. And he wasn't going to help himself. She determined to make sure their project would save his grade and ensure he'd pass the class. *If his transfer grades are strong enough, this project will guarantee she can't sabotage graduation.*

It was awful watching her antagonize him every class. Nell found herself cringing every time Ms. Yashar called Tru's name.

"Tru, I'm sure you have an answer? No? Can someone help Mr. Pitre. He's lost."

"I seem to be missing your work again, Tru. Are you planning to be with me again in the fall?"

"Tru, what are you doing?" (This time, he was reading silently, and yet she felt compelled to address him.)

The berating continued through each class and with each address, Tru was ever polite in his "Yes, ma'am," "No, ma'am," "Excuse me, ma'am?" responses. It sickened Nell. It amused the class – especially the Pom Pom Posse who snickered or added their own commentary to the abuse.

"Come on Tru, entertain us. You see she's ready for a show."

"I can't believe he calls her ma'am."

"He's gonna come for her if she keeps it up. She better watch it."

But Tru did not react in kind. He ignored his classmates. And only when he was inspired to lighten the tension between himself and an attack did his Chaplin routines commence.

They continued to meet after class, but only to set meeting times for the library. Sometimes, Nell would drive them both to the library. Tru, however, said he preferred the walk because it gave him time to clear his head and unwind.

"I know exactly what you mean," Nell agreed. "I ride my bike or drive the long way to my destination for the very same reason."

When it was time to record their public service announcement, Nell was surprised by Tru's knowledge and professionalism. He directed his actor gently but firmly: "Exaggerate the movement. There aren't any words and you are masked, so we have to see bigger movements to know what you're doing."

When they filmed the unmasking, he demanded specific makeup, insisting that colors be bolder and brighter. He helped select the wardrobe (Nell had gotten permission to borrow pieces from Aidan's closet at Chay's house). Specific colors looked better on camera, Tru said, and certain pieces had better movement. Even as he maneuvered his gimbal to record the still images he would later splice together, he was precise about object placement and backgrounds.

He was impressive and Nell was confident in his work. Even as he took their raw footage to edit, she knew the project was stellar. There was clearly going to be no way Ms. Yashar could cast an unfair grade on him.

Tru

The presentation assembly is in two days. It took me awhile to splice the film, but it is just what Nell and I planned. I'm pretty confident that she hasn't said one word to her parents about the showcase. It aint right, Nell's estrangement. She is a visitor in her own home and the Necahuals? Strangers masquerading as parents. Isn't like the first major rule of parenting to nurture their child as she tries to find herself in the world? Or maybe there is some kind of Hippocratic Oath – do no harm or something?

I've thought about how it must be for her. Often. I wanna walk right up to them and say "Lia, Andreas – you failed." It sounds so white bread, so tame, when really so much more can be said about just how crappy these parents are.

Connecting the clues in Nell's moleskin to what she told me wasn't hard. How they forced Aidan out of their home. The man wanted acceptance – or at least respect – and instead he got eviction papers. Rejected right and left by friends *and family*? Aint no reputation worth turning away from your own kid.

In her sketchbook, Nell had drawn Aidan and Chay under one of those wedding arches – a chuppah, I think they're called. From what she said about him, it didn't seem like his style. I don't think Nell went to their nuptials. None of his family attended.

I get it, they could not accept Aidan for who he was. But after he died, I would expect the Necahuals to step up their game. Hell, to start playing it.

Nell's best friend — her big brother — is dead. It's clear she hasn't finished grieving. Beyond noticing the black wardrobe and the somber mood, it should be evident that she's retreated into herself. Do they know she speaks to no one? Do they care?

I don't even remember what we were talking about when she initially told me that Chay still lived in the house he shared with Aidan. She's not allowed to visit him, so when we stopped by to ask for his help on our film, it was risky. She told me that she had defied her father's mandate a few times before, until he confronted her one time when she returned home.

"For a little while after he left my room, I wondered how he'd known where I was. Then it hit me. You know those tracking devices? There's one connected to my phone line."

She told me her father monitors her coming and going. No support. No trust.

So I got a crucial stop I wanna make. I think it's about time someone speak to the Necahuals. I didn't tell Nell my plan. She might've tried to dissuade me. I hope she don't see this as interference. Or, that she'll forgive my intrusion.

Nell told me she goes to the library or rides her bike along the trails until it's almost too dark to see her way home. Ever since she realized the tracker, she's ditched her phone at home. I'm not one-hundred on where she lives, but Zeke's girl, Mo, used to live on a neighboring street in an area they call the Summit - fitting for a family who wants to conform to the norm at any cost.

Walking into the community is like stepping onto the set of Edward Scissorhands or Pleasantville — 1950s idyllic or somethin'. Perfectly cut grass - I think they call them manicured lawns - with those fancy-cut hedges. Uniform. Everyone here must use the same mower. Wait, no — this neighborhood is the one from Stepford Wives, and that would explain so much about Mr. and Mrs. Necahual.

I've walked several blocks scanning the yards for name plaques. The neighborhood does not disappoint. "Welcome: the Joneses." "Parker Family." "Smiths." "Williams." Some of the names are on mailboxes. Others are on hanging signs over porches.

Finally, I see it: "Necahual" painted in small letters on the post of a mailbox. The house is covered in pale bricks with dark green trim. A flag in the garden that lines the cobblestone walkway says "Welcome." The irony of the greeting isn't lost on me. How can they invite in strangers and reject the familiar? The front porch is large and wraps around the house — a wooden swing with plush cushions hangs under it. The oversized door has smoked glass panes etched in gold. One of those large brass knockers adorns the center, but it must be decorative because there's a doorbell with a camera and intercom speaker on the side.

Brace yourself, Tru. This could go wrong with a quickness. I choose the knocker — give it two swift bangs. I learned some time ago that I should back up so as to be seen, so I step to the edge of the porch and stand as straight as I can. I gotta look confident even if I don't feel it.

Minutes tick by. I know someone's home. A car is in the drive. Finally, the shadow of a large man appears to approach, as the muffled voices of at least two people grow louder.

The door opens.

"What can I do for you?" Mr. Necahual stands with his chest puffed out and shoulders squared. His eyes scan me as he speaks.

I'm usually pretty chill when it comes to people's parents, but this guy is intimidating. "Hello, sir. My name is Tru." I say, extending my hand. "Tru Pitre. I'm a school mate of Nell's."

He scrutinizes my outstretched hand but does not take it. I'm left standing with my hand awkwardly reaching toward him.

"Tru?"

"Yes, sir. I've been working with Nell on a project for our English class... maybe she has told you about it?"

"A project? No."

I'm still standing there and I can't help but shuffle my weight. This is not good. "Well, I – we have been working to create a short film for our final project. It's nearly finished now. I'd like to... uh... to invite you and Mrs. Necahual to the school for our presentation."

He's staring at me, one eyebrow raised. Then, heaving audibly, he steps back and ushers me inside with a wave of the hand.

"Can I offer you a coffee? A tea? Water or juice?" He says it begrudgingly, extending a hospitality out of obligation.

"Sir? I am sorry if I'm interrupting your evening." I realize he's offered me a drink, but I'm not sure I want to prolong this house call. He grabs a cola and a glass, sets them on the dark marble counter and is filling the bottom of the glass with rum. He adds the soda and two ice cubs that rattle in the glass as he slowly swirls it. He settles onto the counter stool and pats the one next to him. I take it.

Clearing his throat, he takes a sip of his drink. "Tru, you said? I'm sure you know Nell is not too fond of me right now."

"No, sir. I think she'd really appreciate you coming to see her work."

"So she hasn't told you, then." He says it as a confirmation.

I'm trying not to stare at him, but if my eyes start surveying the room, I'm sure I'll look suspicious. Right now, he's looking absently toward the backsplash of the stove. His hair is grey at the roots, cut into the close-cropped look with the bangs in front that Caesar made famous. His hands are calloused – not the hands of a lawyer or doctor, but those of a man used to manual labor. I realize I don't know what the Necahaul family business is. He's dressed in dark pants and a mock turtle neck shirt – not the typical clothes of a laborer but, maybe, those of the boss?

Too much silence divides us, so I speak up. "I'm not sure what you mean. I just... it's going to be a really good program."

"Does she *know* you're inviting us?"

"Well, no."

"Uh huh."

"Sir, it's part of the senior showcase. There'll be so many parents there."

"Tru, where did you say you're from?"

"I don't believe I did." Why does this matter? I'm thinking he's not seeing this visit as one from a platonic friend. "Nell and I were assigned as partners for this project. We've worked now for several weeks on Nell's script."

"So *you* are the reason she's coming home late?"

Whoa.

"No sir, I don't think so. We work in class or meet at the library."

Mrs. Necahual calls from somewhere nearby. "Andreas, who is it?"

"A friend of Nell's, Lia."

"Nell has a boyfriend?"

Is it hot in here? I'm sweating, suddenly. I take a chance at being rude and interject. "No, ma'am. I'm a classmate." I hope it didn't sound like I don't like Nell, but I'm not sure. There's no reply and Mrs. Necahual does not appear.

"Young man, I'll consider your invitation. But if Nell wanted us to come, she'd have asked us *herself.*" He stands up then and I follow him to the door and step outside as he opens it. Before I can turn to thank him, he's closed the door and his shadow retreats quickly from the entryway.

I don't know what to make of it. He's a special kind of distant – a gruff man with a cold demeanor. I mean, yeah, I wasn't expected, but that reception was unreal. I can only hope they'll decide to support Nell and show up. And that they don't mention that I was the one who invited them.

Maybe I need to let Chay know Aidan's parents might be in the audience. I could warn him – because let's face it Andreas Necahaul is the kind of unpredictable force that could destroy the whole event if prompted. I can't help but wonder if I am setting up the perfect storm with Aidan's partner and his parents in the same venue.

Nell

The auditorium filled quickly with families and interested faculty. Ms. Yashar had clearly been busy promoting her presentation assembly.

In class, she'd beamed as she announced, "Superintendent Harry has confirmed he'll be in the audience for tonight's program. You all: make me proud!"

She looked at Tru and scowled. "This had best be your best effort."

He didn't bother with a response. Just grabbed his bag and shoved his notebook inside.

Now, Tru paced on the side of the stage. It wasn't like him to be nervous. Nell had never seen his confidence lapse even under the nastiest attacks from Ms. Yashar. And yet here he was wringing his hands together - full of anxious movement.

She gripped the note in her pocket. *Now's as good a time as any.*

"Tru? This is for you." she placed the note into his palm and smiled as she squeezed his hand. "I found her."

He looked confused momentarily, and then his eyes widened. "Jo?"

Nell nodded. "Yep."

She didn't volunteer how she'd done it. It was, after all, quite a process and involved a little snooping. First, she noticed a forwarded letter in Tru's apartment with the city he'd lived in still visible. She had seen Jo's picture in his room. Maybe she was on social media? She searched "Jo Nicolas" online and came up with no hits. Then she got a little creative: anagrams. Writing variations of Jo Nicolas in different letter orders – which took *forever* – she searched for each, hoping one would show a person who looked like Tru's girl. And there she was: NICO SOLJA. She sent the girl a private message and after a few very vague replies, Jo offered to chat directly.

Tru hugged Nell tight. "Thank you," he whispered, "you have no idea.... no idea."

"Yo!" Zeke hollered. He'd been talking to Mo and a few classmates when he saw them embracing.

"Wait. What?" Carrie squealed.

But Tru ignored them, releasing Nell to look at the slip of paper she'd given him.

"It's her address," Nell said, shrugging. "I thought you might like to pen her a verse?"

"Bet." Tru half jogged, half skipped away. Then he stopped suddenly. "Thanks again, Nell. You're the best!"

She gave him a thumbs up. Then he was gone.

"Presentations start in five. Lillian, Marco, you are first. The rest of you, review the program for your orders." Ms. Yashar clapped her hands twice quickly, then click clacked to the center of the stage to check the mic.

Nell settled into a corner backstage, leaning against the cool bricks of the wall. She watched her classmates flit around her, checking their trifold displays and reciting their scripts quietly. Nell was glad she and Tru had decided on a film – the hard work was done.

The chatter in the auditorium was deafening. *I hope Chay made it.*

"So Nell? What's up with you and Tru?" Claire and the Pom Pom Posse stood over Nell. "We saw that *tender* moment." They laughed in sync.

Nell, whose eyes had been closed, looked up. She was silent.

"Hey ladies, Zeke is in the building!" He wrapped his arms around Claire and Sue. The girls, still in unison, turned to fawn over him. Leave it to Zeke to create, and then deflect, attention.

Nell took the distraction as opportunity to slip away. In the hallway outside the auditorium, she spotted Tru. He was sitting on the steps, scribbling on a pad. "How's it going?" she asked.

"Solid. I didn't think I'd be able to find her until the courts cleared my case."

"I think our video is up next."

He looked reluctant to stop his flowing words and sat for a second wiggling his pen and thinking. Then he stood and tucked the pad into his back pocket. "Let's do this."

On stage, Tru took the microphone from the stand. He squinted in the bright stage lights as he quickly surveyed the audience. "Hello. I'm Tru Pitre and this is Nell Necahaul. We've put together a presentation about a topic that is close to our hearts – we hope you enjoy our film."

It played, then the applause erupted as soon as the screen went black and continued as Ms. Yashar walked onto the stage to close the program.

"Weren't these amazing? Let's give all of our seniors a hand." She stood clapping with the crowd for some time before raising a hand to silence them. "Thank you all for coming. There are refreshments in the cafeteria outside." She curtseyed and then waited until the curtain closed. Flipping the microphone off and replacing it on the stand, she surveyed the few students who hadn't rushed to beat the lines for snacks.

Her eyes settled on Tru. "Mr. Pitre, your project surprised me."

Nell bristled, she ran through retorts to defend her partner – and now, her friend.

Ms. Yashar continued. "I didn't expect much. Computers don't 'vibe' with you, right? But here you pair up with Nell and suddenly... a professional product."

That was it. The thinly veiled insult covered with a compliment was as close to an apology as Ms. Yashar was capable of giving.

Tru tipped an imaginary bolero. "Why thank you. Mighty glad you approve." And he walked away.

***

Nell stood next to Tru at the reception. Two women were walking briskly toward them. One, a woman with brown skin slightly lighter than Tru's, was beaming.

"You never disappoint!" She said as she reached them. She was still wearing her work scrubs.

Tru smiled. "Ma, I'd like you to meet Nell, my partner in crime. Nell, this is my leading lady – my mother Stephani Pitre and this beautiful gal here? This is the one and only Mama Vee." He raised Mama Vee's mahogany arm and held it as she danced around him.

"Let's hope it's more partner, less crime, yes?" She laughed heartily. "Hello, Nell-my-love. That was a wonderful video."

"Thank you. I've really enjoyed working with Tru on this project. I don't know how I could've done it without his partnership." She spotted Chay then, adding sugar to his coffee. He wore a retro tweed suit jacket and had rolled his pants, exposing his ankles above his brown leather boat shoes. Nell always admired how well he and Aidan dressed. "If you'll excuse me, I see Chay over there. Tru, I have to say hello."

She walked toward Chay, waving to get his attention. "You came!"

"I wouldn't miss it, Nell-Belle. Aidan would be so proud – and honored – that you picked this PSA." He messed her hair. "Kiddo, you are amazing."

"We think so, too." Mr. Necahaul approached quickly, Mrs. Necahaul following close behind.

"Dad? Mom? I... wow, you're here." She wasn't sure how to react. Her father was smiling. Did he actually *like* the film? Could he even understand?

"Well, yes, we are here," he nodded. "You might've mentioned this whole affair to us yourself, but thankfully we heard about it."

"I'm glad you could come." She looked at Chay and he flashed a quick smile before straightening his posture and erasing all signs of emotion from his face. Nell held her breath, nodded, and decided to do it. "Mom and Dad? I'd like to introduce you to Aidan's widow. This is Charles."

Chay didn't move. His thumbs were casually in his pockets. Tru was frozen as he watched the meeting from a few feet away. They rest of the people in the room seemed to disappear, their chatter an indecipherable buzz as Tru strained to listen to the Necahauls. It seemed like time had stopped. And then, slowly, Mrs. Necahaul stepped toward Chay and pulled him into a gentle hug.

Mr. Necahaul – his face stoic – watched his wife embrace Chay. He touched her shoulder and gently pulled her away. Then he stepped forward with his hand outstretched. "Son, it's nice to meet you."

Ms. Yashar's senior assembly was unreal. Of course, Nell and I nailed it with our video. There was at least one other film, but it was one of those presentations where someone just read a script in front of a camera. No cut scenes, no graphics, no creativity. I get it – not everyone is vying for a career in cinema, but they picked the medium, right?

Most of Teach's classes chose to do the obvious: a trifold poster like those in the high school science fair with problem, solution and resources labeled in each segment. There was lots of talking through the boards ('cause no one could see the writing on those pasted papers – some of which were handwritten and illegible even up close). One group performed a drama about their cause. But our video, which I'm certain Ms. Yashar saved for last when the audience was already writhing in their seats restlessly and yawning, was some of my best work. When the lights dimmed for the video to play, people actually watched. And judging from the few people who stopped us on the way to the reception with congratulations, the message was well received.

I don't even really care what Teach has to say. We *earned* our grade. Solid. But there was a much more important project unfolding that night, and the stakes were far greater.

The Necahauls *came!* The scene played out in front of me was better than any I could've imagined. When Mr. Necahaul took Chay's hand in his and then pulled him into an embrace and clapped his back? It changed Nell's whole demeanor. Acknowledging Chay was just a first step – too late for Aidan, but just in time for Nell.

I can't lie. I don't know what changed in Mr. and Mrs. Necahaul. I hope they thought long and hard about their ignorance and intolerance – that they realized what they'd lost and were gonna lose in Nell.

Can people overcome their bigotry?

I met up with Nell in the hallway at school a few days later. I was taking root leaning against the lockers next to Teach's class tryna avoid going in the room before the other students arrived. Nell was early, too. And wearing a vibrant scarf I'd not seen before. If fashion was supposed to mirror her mood, I think this was her tell.

She told me that when they arrived home after the program, her father sat with her at the kitchen counter.

I picture him sitting there with his glass of iced rum and cola, sipping it slowly as he tastes his words before speaking.

"He *cried*, Tru. In all my years, I've never seen my father emotional. But there he was, with a single tear rolling down his cheek. It took everything in me not to wipe it away, 'cause he might get upset that for that moment, I saw his vulnerability."

Nell said Mr. Necahaul spoke slowly, deliberately. I could hear him as she recalled his words: "I was wrong."

Three words. Nothing more. And she had hugged him in the ensuing silence.

I jai like feel something-something trying to envision the scene. If it wasn't an intimate moment, it woulda made a great opening to a drama.

"It doesn't change the past — not at all. But Tru, I think he might actually make amends for how he treated Aidan."

"Do you think he'll make things right?"

"Time will tell. He's spent years hating, after all. He's buying Aidan a headstone," she was actually smiling as she spoke. "Chay and I picked out the words:

> Aidan Necahaul
>
> A fabulous and loved
>
> Son, Brother, Husband

It's important that it reflect him."

"Fabulous? That's certainly non-traditional."

"It's Aidan's favorite word. But what I'm most proud of is that it acknowledges Chay as his spouse."

If Nell saw this as a start of repairing the damage her parents caused by their rejections, then that's exactly what it was. "Solid, Nell. Happy for ya."

***

Mama Vee's been busy. After we installed the wall mural, she held an art auction to raise money for the rec center programs and managed to hook me up with a few grand toward my restitution. I'm so close to paying it off now.

She also sent my parole officer a report showing my community service hours satisfied. She told me I'm officially done, but I know she aint thinking she's getting rid of me that quick. I'm'a always be up helping my community when I'm home — and the rec is home.

I had another near-encounter with Erik that landed me a black eye — not 'cause he lay hands on me, but because I was ducking out of his scopes and caught the corner of a low hanging tree. Then Erik got himself caught up for a minute, so he's currently sitting in lock up waiting on trial. I didn't hear much about his charges, but expect I'll be long gone in New York when he gets out again.

And his rec center infiltrators? Mama Vee got some locals doing security whenever the rec is open, and they've been real strict on vagrants.

My lawyer sent a letter confirming I'm set to go off to school in the fall without probationary limitations or more courtroom visits holding me back. So to celebrate, Ma and I went thrifting for some dorm stuff. Man the things people send off to second-hand shops is like abandoned treasure! Half the gear I scored still had tags on it.

It's real now. I picked up my cap and gown. There is *nothing* like holding that regalia. Trying to fit that cap over my twists was a challenge, but I look good in it as I stand in the mirror admiring myself. I just need a shape-up and I'm ready to walk across that stage and take my diploma.

Nell is speaking at graduation, a valedictory address to the graduates. She's hella nervous. Aint no doubt she'll thrive up there in the spotlight, nerves or not.

It's been a minute since I sent off my letter to Jo. I still don't know how Nell got ahold of her to find an address, but I'm grateful she did (even if it means she was snooping in my business). Nell's got me rethinking my no ties clause. She is cool and I'd like to stay in touch even after I move out of here.

Anyway, I've been stalking the mailbox for a response. The mailman knows me now – at first he wasn't too keen on me leaning up against the mailbox waiting for him to roll up e'ry day. He looked at me hard, obviously trying to determine if I was up to no good. But I wasn't tryna steal nobody's bills when mine is piled up. Even though I stood there, he put the mail into the box as he said hello. I guess he got used to me after the first few times, 'cause now he knows my unit and will sidestep the box and give me my stuff directly.

I'm waiting now, standing here with the sun rays baking me. The mail truck is a few rows down the street, but I can see it from here. Blinking caution lights warn those behind him that he's moving slow – so slow – and stopping often. I know I'm pro'lly gonna be disappointed when he hands me the stack of "Current Resident" letters and advertisements, but I'm 'a wait anyway.

Finally, he pulls up to my mailbox. He puts the truck in park and flips through the sorted mail he's got sitting in the center bin to his left.

Why is he stalling? He gives new meaning to snail mail with his pace.

I can smell the letter even before he hands it to me. It's Jo's strawberries and cream scent that she spritzes on everything – like a baptism in scented mist. The nostalgia that smell gives me – The late nights at the park, shooting the breeze while slowly swinging back and forth on the 'set or settling down on the wide top of the slide where during the day the kids played royals overseeing their domain. Evenings spent chillin' in one of our apartments, Jo sitting on the couch with one leg tucked under her and me with my arm thrown across the back of the couch. Inside, one of our Mas would serve up somethin' good, setting it on the sofa table with our red plastic cups of juice. Sometimes that smell would go home with me – on my jacket after a hug goodnight – and it'd stay with me while I did my homework at my desk.

I would've expected those strawberries and cream to be faint after the trip through the sorting machines and on the airplane or boats or whatever it traveled in to get to its final destination, but it didn't. My heart is beating fast. I aint never been this excited to get a response from somebody – not even after sending off my college application.

Mailman hands me the envelop – it's oversized and a pale lavender color. Even though there's no sender's name, she's got her address written in the corner in her bubbly print. I can't even wait 'til I'm inside to read what Jo has to say, so I sit on the landlord's stoop. I'm so tempted to tear into the envelop, but I restrain myself and slide my key under the flap to loosen the adhesive.

I hold my breath as I pull out the letter from my friend.

Names and Meanings

I'm a firm believer that name meanings can have power. Because of this, I chose character names that I felt fit the persona of each.

Necahual - survivor
      Nell - champion
      Aidan – fire (Celtic/Gaelic)
      Andreas – warrior (Greek)
      Aemelia – rival (Latin)

Pitre - clown
      Tru - true
      Stephani – crown (French)

Nicolas – people
      Jo' - victory

Erik - always/one & ruler (Norse)

Yashar – honest
      Chava – life (Hebrew)

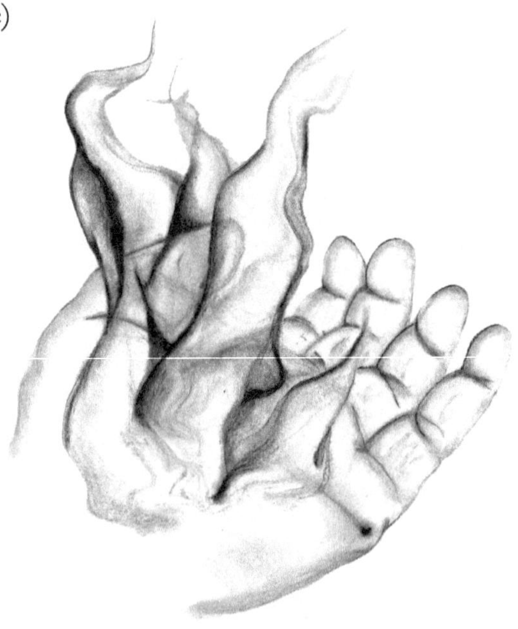

An Interview with Tru Pitre

Q: What is your idea of perfect happiness?

A: **Man, I jus' wanna get back to freedom. Tryin' to do right by my mom isn't easy when everything is stacked against me.**

Q: What is your greatest fear?

A: **I haveta protect my rep - it's all I got.**

Q: What is the trait you most deplore in yourself?

A: **I'm smart - really smart - but that doesn't win fans.**

Q: What is the trait you most deplore in others?

A: **People who don't know how easy they got it.**

Q: Which living person do you most admire?

A: **Ma.**

Q: What is your greatest extravagance?

A: **We don't have much. I aint extravagant with nuthin' but my dreams.**

Q: What is your current state of mind?

A: **Blown. I'm real tired of being their clown.**

Q: What do you consider the most overrated virtue?

A: **Being the life of the party.**

Q: On what occasion do you lie?

A: **Seems like e'ryday.**

Q: What do you most dislike about your appearance?

A: **I'm noticed *all the time*. It's hard to go unnoticed when you look like me.**

Q: Which living person do you most despise?

A: **Her father. It's his fault all this happened.**

Q: What is the quality you most like in a man?

A: **Humility.**

Q: What is the quality you most like in a woman?

A: **Sincerity.**

Q: Which words or phrases do you most overuse?

A: **Dunno. I'm versatile. Gotta keep 'em guessin.**

Q: What or who is the greatest love of your life?

A: **I'm learnin' I gotta love myself before I can love others**

Q: When and where were you happiest?

A: **Before my case caught me up and ruined all I'd built.**

Q: Which talent would you most like to have?

A: **I'm fire with computers... but I don't use 'em. I wanna be invisible.**

Q: If you could change one thing about yourself, what would it be?
A: **I cared.**
Q: What do you consider your greatest achievement?
A: **I stood up for what was right even though it burned me.**
Q: If you were to die and come back as a person or a thing, what would it be?
A: **I don't buy into reincarnation. One life - make it count.**
Q: Where would you most like to live?
A: **In a city that never sleeps. I hate the dark.**
Q: What is your most treasured possession?
A: **Her picture.**
Q: What do you regard as the lowest depth of misery?
A: **Being misunderstood.**
Q: What is your favorite occupation?
A: **Computers were my thing. Now, it's all about makin' films and tellin' the story.**
Q: What is your most marked characteristic?
A: **Uh... humor?**
Q: What do you most value in your friends?
A: **I aint had a friend in a minute.**
Q: Who are your favorite writers?
A: **Come on, you know I aint reading.**
Q: Who is your hero of fiction?
A: **...**
Q: Which historical figure do you most identify with?
A: **Charlie Chaplin and Tupac Shakur (different reasons, same respect due)**
Q: Who are your heroes in real life?
A: **Ma. She's my roots and my sunshine.**
Q: What are your favorite names?
A: **Mine. You have to admit "Tru" has a ring to it.**
Q: What is it that you most dislike?
A: **Fake. Phony. Fraudulent.**
Q: What is your greatest regret?
A: **Getting caught.**
Q: How would you like to die?
A: **Living.**
Q: What is your motto?
A: ***Reality is wrong. Dreams are for real.*** **(That's from Tupac, not me.)**

Acknowledgements

I've been looking forward to writing this page, and dreading writing this page for some time. There are so many people who were critical to me arriving at this moment and I don't want to miss anyone.

Rob, I thank you. For sharing in the creation of Tru. For countless hours listening to sentences, then paragraphs, then pages (and again). For forcing me to believe in the story – in the lives of my characters. For your never-waning support of this project.

Mom, my best friend and my forever confidant. Thank you for having confidence in me even when I lacked it in myself. Thank you for listening patiently and without judgement as I lamented the writing process and struggled to find my words.

Daddy, you cheer for me in the streets better than anyone I know. Thank you for spreading the news.

RiAnne and Yadon, I appreciate you. For giving me the time to write, for sharing my joy in the creation, and for joining in as my writing buddies with your own creativity.

LauraChioma, I'm indebted to you. For taking my ideas on the cover and interior art and making it amazing. For checking my sketches and adding your own. For reminding me that tenacity is a necessary trait.

Rico and J.D., I carry you with me.

My students, I see you. I respect you. And I hope you continue to reach for those dreams and live in love. You inspire me daily.

Dr. Melinda Clayton, thank you for encouraging me to press on. For believing in Tru and Nell. For assuring me that superfluous words were not.

Professors Josh Berk and Tiffany Trent, and my SNHU MFACW classmates, your discussions during the early outlines and character sketches were invaluable. Thanks for being a part of the process.

Colleagues, where would I be without you? The love, the post shares, and the excitement give me all the feels. I am grateful for your support of this new chapter in my career.

Tru Untrue is the debut novel of **Rachelle Jones Smith**.

Rachelle never got her fill of high school, so she goes back daily. After class, she's usually found writing, photographing, or pursuing adventures. Years ago, she took her driver's test sitting on phone books to see over the steering wheel, but a lot has changed since then. Phone books are digital and seats that rise make road trips with her husband and children awesome and a lot less dangerous!

She tries to write fiction with strong young adult characters and hopes her YA work will inspire, comfort, and relate to people on all walks of life.

Rachelle studied comic book art, journalism, criminal justice and creative writing in school.

In Your Dreams

TOTEM

"When my mom first left," Joshua began. "It was on a trip to build educational centers for still-isolated tribal communities."

He held up a small token in his palm — a talisman with woven threads of hair jutting from the wood figure.

"She sent this to me at Pap's a few weeks into her trip with an elaborate letter."

He was talking softly now, less to her than himself, eyes looking upwards as he coaxed his memories.

In the few moments of pause, Minerva poured the boy another mug of cocoa. He needed to talk. The grandchild of her elderly neighbors seemed to have no one to confide in and she, without a child of her own, welcomed him into her home regularly for afternoon chats. If she'd had a son, he'd probably be about the same age as Joshua. And today, this young man seemed to be reaching out to her for help. There was clearly something on his mind.

He stroked the smooth belly of the large-eyed figure.

"'I had this blessed by the village shaman for you,' she wrote. 'If you rub it and think of me, our spirits will link in our dreams.'" He surprised himself with an awkward, involuntary chuckle. "I believed her so *desperately.* I *wanted* my mom home. I *needed* her to come back."

Looking down at the carving, he traced the crude depression of nostrils and lips.

Minerva studied the figure in his hands and felt ill-at-ease. She shuddered.

Joshua was waiting for her to coax him to continue, she realized, as his tear-filled eyes met hers.

"She did her best to keep in touch, right?" Minerva said. "It couldn't have been easy being so far from you."

He nodded. "No. I'm pretty sure she wanted me with her." Sipping the cocoa, he was quiet, lost in his memories.

Minerva didn't dare intrude. Instead, she sat across from him at her kitchen table and savored her cup of tea.

***

She'd included a photograph with the letter, a black and white photo still smelling of the chemical fixatives of a home darkroom. He'd inhaled that smell trying to make her tangible. In the image, she was dressed in a flowing dress, her hair was wrapped in clothe except for a few dark strands that blew across her smiling mouth. She looked so happy, casually brushing at the hair with a finger and holding a parchment in the other hand that hung loosely at her side. Behind her were several make-shift structures – some tent-like made of paperbark and leafy material, others mud brick and grass. A few dark-skinned children, bare-chested and lost in a frozen game of chase, appeared blurred at one side of her. She was barefoot on the clay earth.

Grandmom read over his shoulder as he savored his mother's letter. In it, she described with meticulous care the witch doctor who'd crafted the figurine, apologizing for not including a picture of him in the package.

Here, they don't believe in photographs. Cameras steal a piece of your soul and the image created carries it within. He called my camera a wicked thief and forbade me from turning it toward him.

Oh, I wish you could see him! He's a character worthy of one of your paintings. He has thick hair in coiled tendrils that have collected the elements, including a clay he uses to bind the white locks together. Black-as-night pupils sit deep in amber eyes that I'm sure can take of your soul if you look at him straight. His skin is a deep sienna brown, his nose is broad and lips are full. His face is etched with age, his limbs slightly gnarled with ailment. But he is a lively man, bent shorter than his height, though agile and full of history.

During rituals, he wears a medallion made of plant materials. It is woven in a circular pattern and decorated with kangaroo teeth. -- The roos are here in abundance and they are funny creatures - - He holds a bowl carved of wood, the etched sides show indigenous animals and flowers. A red-purple liquid is swirled slowly around the bowl's interior before being set above an open-flame pit. His hand flicks powder into the bowl, sending the liquid into a bubble. The fire sputters protest when the bubbles rise-up and fall onto the charred logs. I don't dare say I know what this ritual is for, but soon, they will have the rites for the young people here to become adults.

This totem I am sending you is special. I chopped the wood myself from a tree shortly after we arrived in the tradition here. The engraving is me and the hair is made of feather down, animal fur and strands of my own hair. Hold it and think of me — it is a link to my spirit while I am away *from you. Here, dreams are sacred to creation. We can meet in*

our dreams.

Mom

    Grandmom reached this passage at the same time he had, and she huffed before swiping the parchment from him. "Foolery. Nonsense. Dream links? My daughter – your mother – has... Uggh. We'll have none of this, you here?"

    Protectively, he clutched the figurine tighter as she crumbled the letter and set it in the waste basket. When she'd moved further away to do the dishes, he slid from his chair at the kitchen table, retrieved the letter, and retreated to his room.

    That night, he rubbed the totem and stroked its hair. He closed his eyes and whispered, "I love you, mom," as he placed the figure carefully under his pillow.

    In his dreams, she came to him, arriving to arrange his blankets and kiss his forehead. " And I love you. It's you and me forever. I'm here when you need me, " she said, as she switched off his bedside lamp.

And Then She Was Gone

His eyes swelled with tears and his lips quivered slightly in the corner. He raked a hand through his chestnut hair, disturbing the curl with finger trails.

"Mom is dead," he repeated carefully, holding each word on his tongue and practicing it before pronouncement. "Mom."

He looked at the assembly in the small, cluttered office. VP Nichols sat nervously and busied himself separating his collared shirt from his flushed neck and clearing his throat as if preparing to deliver a speech. And Grandmom and Pap — their hands clutched between them, he perched on the edge of the chair and she slumped toward him in her own chair looking very much like she might slip to the floor and disappear. He wanted to disappear, too.

Was mom ever even sick?

It'd been so long since he'd heard from her. A quick call on Christmas Eve. "Hey bub, just calling to say I love you. Now get to bed before Santa skips the house," she said. He could hear the hurry up in her voice. "Oh, and, uh… there's something special under the tree from me." Then the line was silent except for his breathing. He muttered "Yeah, ma" and waited for the click to deaden the call.

"I… gotta finish my chem test," he muttered absently, but he made no real effort to stand. He couldn't — his legs were missing. His whole body was gone. He was watching the sad scene from outside himself.

Dead. No more sporadic calls from wherever the work was that year. No more promises to visit during school break or to fly him out to her. Grandmom and Pap were it. So much for "you'll just stay here for a few months while I get settled."

"My test —" someone says something, he thought, save me. He looked to his Grandmom dabbing her eyes with a balled-up tissue and looked quickly away.

He concentrated on the voices from the outer office: "You don't understand. She was taking pictures of me and posting them on SnapChat. I saw it." "Yeah, I took my phone back. He ain't allowed to snatch it from me. So? It's my property. Stupid teacher." "One more tardy and that's Saturday school for you."

Finally. VP Nichols broke the awkward silence of the stuffy office. "I think it's better to postpone that test, Joshua."

Pap reached for his cane and stood. "Yes. Yes."

Joshua looked down to where his hands had settled on his phone. Flicking it on with his fingerprint, he scanned the notifications. For a second, he thought about posting to his story, something like 'Thought today couldn't suck more. Just found out Mom's dead' with a coffin emoji and a shot of the floor.

He decided against it. He didn't want the sympathy, anyway.